THE SILENT SISTER

C.L. JENNISON

BLOODHOUND BOOKS

SUNDAY 26TH OCTOBER 1997

Rubie flicks her glossy black mane over her bare, sun-kissed shoulders as Scarlet creeps awkwardly up the long, gravelled driveway. Rubie tuts and huffs impatiently, rotating her arm exaggeratedly in a "hurry up" gesture as the many bangles on her wrists jangle. Her sister finally joins her at the entrance to the farmhouse clutching two pairs of red strappy sandals. She stands like a flamingo, pressing the sole of her left foot against her right calf and wincing.

'You took your time,' Rubie stage-whispers, clamping her hands on her hips. 'Did either of them see you?'

Scarlet shakes her head and straightens up, grinning now.

'Come on then. The party started ages ago, and we've got a twenty-minute walk yet.'

Scarlet's smile slips as she looks back at their home, backlit by the full moon already visible in the darkening sky. The farmhouse itself – a sturdy albeit tired residence, its two mismatched extensions tacked onto the back and side in a Frankenstein-inspired design – seems as though it's asleep. No lights on, no movement from its occupants within.

'What if Rosalie tells on us?' she asks.

Rubie rolls her carefully kohl-lined eyes. The result of a *Just Seventeen* step-by-step make-up look. 'You just said neither her nor Mum saw you sneak out. They definitely didn't see me, so what's to tell?' She shrugs then roughly grabs Scarlet's wrist and starts walking, pulling her sister along behind her, their feet shoved into old, flat ballet shoes in preparation for the walk across the fields to the party nearer the middle of town. 'Anyway, I'm sure I heard Rosie snivelling in her room earlier,' Rubie throws back to Scarlet. 'Probably caught her reflection in the mirror and realised what a manky troll she looks like with that hideous haircut.'

'She hates us so much she doesn't even want to look like us anymore,' says Scarlet.

Rubie thinks she detects a rare sympathetic tone in her sister's voice and stops walking. She drops Scarlet's wrist and turns to her. 'We might be sisters, Scar, but she doesn't look like us anyway, not really. Not up close. And especially not now with that hack-job hairdo. *We* were given Mum and Dad's superior genes in the womb. And tonight, we look hotter than ever!' She pouts her shiny red lips to emphasis the point.

Scarlet's smile returns easily. 'Felton's eyes are going to pop out of his head when he sees you, Rube.'

Rubie has fantasised about that exact moment several times already. 'I know,' she says, so assured, so excited, so determined to claim her man. 'Now come on, before that bimbo Kayleigh gets to him first!'

Twenty minutes later, they reach the party, their bare legs slightly red and itchy after cutting across the familiar fields and through the long, prickly grass. But better that than surely suffering sprained or broken ankles if they'd attempted the straightforward route in their four-inch platform heels. Plus, they'd no doubt have been spotted by one or more of the gossipy town fishwives. Both fortunately and unfortunately, the sisters are hard to miss.

After changing into their strappy sandals and stashing their flats under the hedge bordering the paved, curved driveway, they begin sashaying, albeit steadily, towards Kayleigh's parents' grand house.

Although it's Kayleigh's end-of-summer party, Rubie and Scarlet have decided to treat it as their birthday bash too, to celebrate turning seventeen in a few days. One year away from getting out of Stonethorpe-On-Sea for good. They've already made a pact, a sacred, sisterly, blood pact that on their eighteenth birthdays, they're leaving the virtually comatose town behind. As well as Rosalie, who's always been odd, not just the odd one out. They sneered about her while they got ready, smearing gloopy gloss on each other's lips, brushing their long black hair until it shone, and selecting matching off-the-shoulder tops to wear with their choker necklaces and black miniskirts.

The thrill of successfully sneaking out and actually making it to the party strums silently within Rubie, and within Scarlet too, she's sure of that. She can *feel* it as though their bodies and souls are one. Their ailing mother's gentle disappointment is only a distant possible consequence right now, to be dealt with as and when. Whatever happens, they'll stick together, as they always do and have always done. Maybe they'll even find a way to blame their daring disobedience on Rosie.

Scarlet reaches for Rubie's hand as they approach the "Dallas Ranch", as their mum always calls it, and they interlink their fingers. It's the poshest house in town, double-fronted and symmetrical, like a child's drawing depiction of a perfect home. The palatial residence lures them inside, the chorus of Meredith Brooks's 'Bitch' aptly blasting from its belly.

The wide front door is opened just as they reach it, and a

gang of giggling revellers bustle out. A gangly, spotty boy turns and blatantly ogles them both with bloodshot eyes, sporting a lascivious grin. Rubie recognises him from school and playfully winks back. He laughs freely, throwing his head back, his prominent Adam's apple bobbing, before one of his mates reaches out and drags him away, shouting about heading to Sandy Crest, the local caravan park.

Moving onwards, Rubie and Scarlet slip into the hallway of the impressive house. The music is so loud it feels as though the walls are vibrating and Rubie stops for a few seconds to take in the atmosphere. Straight ahead, a staircase littered with can- and bottle-carrying partygoers arcs gently towards the first floor and an archway to the left frames a view of an open-plan living area, also teeming with fellow teenagers, either chatting, laughing, drinking or snogging. The double doors to her right are closed. Rubie wonders if Kayleigh's parents are squirrelled away behind them, or upstairs somewhere, or whether they've trusted their popular seventeen-year-old daughter with hostess duties alone. Either way, the party is in full swing and there are no adults in sight.

Rubie feels Scarlet squeeze her hand and she squeezes back her reassurance as they move through the throng deeper into the house, slinking and swaying their bodies in time with the music, ignoring loaded stares and insincere smiles from judgemental ex-schoolmates. Teenage hostility and judgement at its finest. But Rubie doesn't care; she's used to it now. She and Scarlet and Rosalie are the local curiosities: identical triplets who live in the most remote, ramshackle farmhouse on the outskirts of the seaside town. Their sporadic school attendance and prickly personalities since their father died and their mother's health nosedived have all but alienated them from their peers during the past two and a half years. If it wasn't for knowing Kayleigh since primary school, they wouldn't have been invited to this party at all.

However, being out socially – and secretly – is such a novelty that Rubie is determined to enjoy herself. She's thankful that Uncle Silas went back last weekend because if he was still here and found out they'd snuck out to a sinful house party, especially on a Sunday, she and Scarlet would have had to kiss goodbye to being allowed to go to the Halloween fair before it leaves on Friday. As long as they get back home and into their bedroom without disturbing their mum, or alerting Rosie to their return, they'll be as free as birds.

As they navigate through the big, busy kitchen and into a humid, packed conservatory overlooking a huge garden decorated with fairy lights, the DJ segues seamlessly from the Spice Girls's 'Wannabe' to Take That's 'Relight My Fire'. The crowd whoops and Rubie is suddenly swept forward in a surge of movement. She totters on her heels but Scarlet swiftly steadies her and points towards the garden.

The atmosphere crackles with a heady mix of tension and excitement as a group of older boys suddenly appear at the sliding doors separating the conservatory from the wraparound patio. Jaws drop collectively as they step inside, all brooding expressions, confident gaits and short-sleeved T-shirts despite the now cool October night. Rubie thinks they look like a cool boy band and half expects them to whip out microphones and start singing along with the track while running their hands through their hair and grabbing their crotches. The gall of them is intoxicating to her. It seems to be for the majority of the rammed room too.

Scarlet squeezes the top of her arm. 'It's the Cliftons and the other hot boys from the fair,' she screams into Rubie's ear, unnecessarily. Rubie nods, not taking her eyes from the ringleaders and brothers Felton and Colton Clifton. Red-haired

Felton is the tallest, sporting the earring and the floppy fringe. He's running the pad of his thumb across his bottom lip and surveying the scene while the rest – all dark-haired except dirty-blond Colton – slap each other playfully and eyeball the crowd appreciatively.

Rubie vividly recalls setting hungry eyes on Felton last Friday afternoon after she and Scarlet took a detour on the way home from town to have a neb at the fair workers setting up before opening night on Saturday, as was their tradition. Both Rubie and Scarlet loved watching the rangy, muscled man-boys erecting the rides, laying the electric cables, and moving and carrying equipment. They both loved hearing their strange verbal shorthand, imagining their tongues wrapped around words spoken exclusively to them, ideally before their tongues wrapped around something else entirely. They were ready for it. For proper first kisses, for lean but toned arms slung around their skinny shoulders, for finding out what working man's hands and fingers on their virgin skin felt like...

Kayleigh appears like magic at Rubie's side, eyes wide and cheeks rosy at the sight of the gate-crashers. Despite her apparent shock, Rubie detects a flutter of excitement within her old friend. The Cliftons deigning to descend on her party is going to elevate her status even further in the teenage Stonethorpe-On-Sea community.

Since their arrival a few months ago, the enigmatic Clifton boys have been a source of great interest to most of the girls in the small town despite, or probably because of, the adults' disapproval of the fair and the chaos it always brings. Every October they descend, boosting tourism in the off-season, but boosting the crime rate too. There's been talk of a petition banning them for years, which has yet to be realised. Something Rubie is extremely grateful for.

The crowd parts and Felton sidles up to Kayleigh. He gives her an appreciative once-over, generating an even deeper blush.

'This your bash?' he asks. Kayleigh nods and smiles her belated invitation in return.

He leans down to briefly kiss her cheek and the whole room erupts, cheering and hollering over the music, elated that they're now at the coolest party of their lives so far.

Rubie's stomach flips as Felton steps back from Kayleigh and throws a glance her way. It's as magical as she imagined. He raises one eyebrow, and she makes a pact with herself: before this party ends, she's going to have her first proper kiss – and maybe more – and it's going to be with him. Tonight is going to be the start of the rest of her life.

FRIDAY 27TH OCTOBER 2017

CHAPTER TWO

ALLIE

Ebony's name flashes up on my phone as I'm driving, and I sigh heavily. I detest first names that are colours and true to her moniker, Ebony feels like a black cloud following me about, metaphorically hovering above my head, ready to drench me with her snippily delivered instructions. Despite the fact that I've already ghostwritten two moderately successful books for our boss, Ralph Delaney of Delaney Publishing, she can't just leave me to it. In her case, PA stands for "perpetual annoyance" rather than "personal assistant" and I can't wait to be done with her as well as this last book in the dull-as-ditchwater *Forgotten Fairground* series.

Ralph himself is not so bad, but I just want to be free to write what I want to write without having to be micromanaged by the infuriating Ebonys of the world. But first, I need to get this job done so I can get paid and dig myself out of the deep financial hole I'm currently in. It's fucking expensive being me, especially now I'm about to be homeless due to Claudia breaking up with me.

It's an effort but I manage to keep my tone civil as I answer

Ebony's call. It's the second time she's rung during the two-and-a-half-hour car journey.

'Are you nearly there yet, Allie? I'm just about to jump on a call with Ralph and I need to update him on your ETA,' she says.

I cringe at her use of jargon: "jump on a call" and "ETA". She uses phrases like these all the time, as though she's swallowed a corporate wanker phrasebook. I suspect she loves pestering people unnecessarily. My annoyance flares yet again but I check the satnav dutifully.

'I'm about thirty minutes away now,' I confirm.

'And did you get a chance to read through all the articles and documents I forwarded to you?'

She sent them through about an hour ago – whilst I was driving.

'I had a quick look at one or two when I pulled into a service station. I'll go through them all thoroughly tonight after I check in to the B&B,' I reply.

She actually tuts but what am I supposed to do – read and drive at the same time? I'd be able to if Ralph's location budget had stretched to a driver too, but it hadn't. Besides, I like the solitude of travelling alone, so much so I volunteered to make my own way here instead of navigating multiple trains, as Ebony would have had me do. Being stuck inside a contained space with the general public is definitely not my idea of pleasant.

'Hmm... okayyy,' she says, drawing out the word. I can picture her inspecting her perfect manicure. Her signature colour is black, of course. 'Remember that they're just a jumping off point and Ralph is expecting plenty more research, especially horse's mouth accounts from relevant parties.'

'Yes, I know,' I reply through gritted teeth.

'I don't need to remind you he's trusting you with this.'

'No, you don't, Ebony.' I roll my eyes in exasperation.

We've already been through this, in the meeting we had in London a couple of weeks ago, in which I found out I was being dispatched to Stonethorpe-On-Sea on an extra all-expenses-paid fact-finding mission for the third and final book in Ralph's riveting series. ("Riveting" being Ebony's arse-licking adjective and far from accurate. And that's not me being overly critical either – I'm a great ghostwriter but there's only such much I can do with unriveting content.) My insistence that I could do it all remotely from my home in Leeds fell on deaf ears due to Ralph's belief – and Ebony's of course – that face-to-face interviews and personal accounts would add an extra dimension to the book and that a focus on "downsides" and "controversy" would boost sales. The controversies in this case being two serious, and still unsolved, attacks in the late nineties during the infamous Halloween fair week. In their wisdom, the permanent residents of the small seaside town determined the transient fair folk were to blame, and from what I've heard and read so far, were successful in banning the fair from visiting the town again from 1999 onwards.

I'm not a journalist so I resent having to do all this extra factual legwork, but Ralph is funding the trip, as well as paying me a generous bonus once the whole series is finished. Even though I'm now mere miles away from Stonethorpe-On-Sea, I'm still seriously conflicted about it. But a few days away might do me good, especially as I don't fancy being home alone in the run up to my birthday, with just my precious ragdoll Story and Rightmove for company. I'd miss Claudia even more than I already do, even though she's given me a strict two-week deadline in which to find a new place to live while she stays with her bitch of a sister in Manchester.

So, being forced to stay in the back end of beyond is preferable to being in familiar surroundings without her – just.

On the other hand, living in a big city brings with it a blanket of anonymity and I'm not keen on inserting myself into a small town with a small-town mentality, albeit temporarily. I hope I can work it to my advantage, get what I need, and get out. Back to my own bed, my cat and my books. The clichéd life of a solitary writer.

I force myself to tune back into Ebony.

'And we'll meet again next Friday, the third of November, here in London, to go over the outline and the first few chapters. I've already booked your overnight stay. You'll be ready?' She phrases this as a question but it's a statement. Another one of her management lingo tricks.

I bite my tongue, sinking my teeth slowly into the tip.

'Allie? Have I lost you?' she immediately interjects into the pause.

'Everything will be ready,' I say, releasing my tongue.

'Good-o!' she replies, and I wince. 'Safe trip. Talk soon.'

She hangs up and I briefly close my eyes, knowing she probably means "talk soon" literally. I lean my head back against the headrest, trying to tame my temper before it erupts. As if the universe knows I need the distraction, my phone buzzes and I see that my neighbour, who's looking after my little furball for a few days while I'm away, has sent me a couple of WhatsApp images of Story looking raggedy and adorable. The picture makes my heart flip and reminds me again of how much my life has changed in the past few months. Claudia brutally ending things and giving me notice to move out of her flat – the home we shared and made cosy together. Her toxic sister Shelley coming to collect her and not bothering to hide her glee that Claudia and I were over. She never liked me and always made me feel like an outcast on the few occasions we did anything as a three. Being the odd one out is the story of my life.

I spend the rest of the journey idly thinking about things I hate as much as I hate Claudia's sister. The list is constantly growing longer but today my brain homes in on jazz music, obvious-looking wigs, multiple sclerosis, and the Leeds housing market. How, at thirty-six years of age, am I still too skint to buy rather than rent, even after my relatively industrious twenties?

I pass the sign announcing I've arrived in Stonethorpe-On-Sea as dusk is descending. The streetlights blink on as I drive past the prom and through the main street, passing a tattoo parlour, a bookies and a chippy, which are all open and brightly lit amongst the other dark blanks in the parade of shops.

I spy the B&B Ebony has booked me into a couple of minutes later – a three-storey property on the end of a row of drab-looking terraces, its old-fashioned vacancies sign illuminated and swaying in the coastal breeze. There are no parking spaces directly outside, so I turn left at the mini roundabout and swing back on myself, finding a spot on the prom facing the sea. The tide is in, and the murky grey water is choppy, reflecting my feelings about being here. Over to the right, a few miles down the road, is the patch of land where the fair I'm researching and writing about was always erected, next to Sandy Crest caravan park. Apparently, that closed down years ago.

Surprisingly, Ebony hasn't called or messaged again yet, so I gather my bag from the passenger seat, retrieve my wheelie case from the boot of the car and walk across the road to the B&B. It looked better in the pictures online, which clearly haven't been updated for a while.

I make my way through the waist-height wrought-iron gate and along the cracked concrete path, noticing that the black paint on the huge bay window frame is peeling. When I reach the porch, I discover that one of the panes of glass in the outer door is sporting a long vertical crack. Due to its state of disrepair, the guest house reminds me of the ramshackle house I grew up in and I'm not exactly enthused about going inside. The phrase "all expenses paid" isn't as impressive as it sounds now that I can see up close exactly what Ralph has paid for. Or rather hasn't paid for. Perhaps this is Ebony's way of syphoning a cut from the budget? I wouldn't put it past her.

The breeze picks up as a couple of seagulls swoop and call and I instinctively touch my hand to my hair, just to make sure it's secure. I can feel it is but it's more of an anxiety tic now that the stress of the break-up has exacerbated my alopecia. I glance back towards the agitated sea, suddenly struck by a monstrous image in my mind's eye: a tsunami rearing up and over the tidal barrier, swallowing everything in its path, including me. Eradicating Stonethorpe-On-Sea completely. But instead of terrifying me, the thought brings me comfort. With a wry smile, I turn back towards the door and step inside.

CHAPTER THREE

ALLIE

The B&B's interior is busy and the assault on my senses does nothing to improve my mood. Patterned carpet, patterned wallpaper and a short, older woman wearing a below knee-length skirt made out of what looks like a retro patterned curtain. She's on her sensibly shod tiptoes dusting the frilled lampshades, which sit wonkily on top of a pair of wall lights. A cloying floral smell hangs heavily in the air, forcing me to take shallow breaths. I drag my wheelie case over the threshold, and she startles, pressing a palm to her ample bosom and emitting an overly dramatic cry as her feather duster quivers.

'Goodness me! You gave me quite the fright there. Lost in my own little world I was.' She chuckles as she regards me more closely. 'Quite the vision in pink waltzing in! Well, as you can see, I do love a bit of colour too.' She bustles behind the wooden reception desk, placing her duster on top, next to a stack of newspapers with a large pebble paperweight on top.

'Allie Sawyer,' I tell her, not acknowledging her reference to my pink hair. 'Booked in until Monday.'

She taps a finger against my name in her page-a-day diary. It's the only one there, which doesn't surprise me; this town isn't exactly a tourist hotspot anymore, and especially during off-season. 'You are indeed, dear. Welcome to Stonethorpe-On-Sea. I'm Marla, your landlady for the next few days. I've given you the front bedroom upstairs. Lovely big bay window with a view to the sea. Breakfast is served at 8am sharp.' She smiles as she hands me an old-fashioned key attached to a tarnished gold disc bearing the number one.

I take it and point towards the staircase behind her. 'This way?' I ask, grabbing the handle of my wheelie case.

'Yes, dear, just the one flight to the first floor. My son would normally play bellboy, but he's got a longer shift at the caff today.' I catch a Northern twang to her voice.

'I can manage,' I say, but before I can even step forward, she continues talking as if I haven't even spoken.

'Such a good boy he is, and to think he was premature.' She clucks her tongue and shakes her head. 'Strapping lad now though. Me and my late husband Bruce said it must have been all the sea air over the years strengthening his lungs.'

I raise my eyebrows in surprise at the overshare. Marla is obviously one of those godawful people who talks at you rather than with you, oblivious to a disengaged expression or an active cue to end the exchange. Something else to add to my hate list. As if to prove my point, she powers on, 'When we moved here in '98, he was just four months old. A little scrap of a thing he was. And now he lugs suitcases up and down stairs for his old mum without even a wheeze.' She beams proudly.

'Right, well, I'll...' I try again to leave.

'Where did you say you were from, dear?'

I didn't say anything, but I choose to oblige her nosiness and answer honestly.

'Leeds!' she echoes. 'What a coincidence! That's where me and my Bruce lived before we moved here. You haven't come too far but far enough for a change of scenery. And are you here for business or pleasure, dear?'

'Work,' I reply bluntly.

Marla wears an expectant expression, clearly waiting for me to elaborate. When I don't, she reaches for her feather duster and dislodges the paperweight from the stack of newspapers revealing a copy of the *Stonethorpe Herald* on top. She notices me glance at the fully revealed headline: *Sanderson Sister Remains Silent*. She tuts.

'Nasty business that,' she says, nodding at the paper and pursing her lips. 'It's been twenty years but it's still a tragic blight on the town's history.'

Now she's caught my interest, so I move forward to take a closer look, work mode activated.

'What happened?' I ask, ready to mentally take notes. I already know quite a bit of the backstory thanks to Ebony's files, but if Ralph wants "horses-mouth accounts", that's what he's going to get.

She immediately leans in and lowers her voice conspiratorially even though we're the only ones here as far as I can tell. 'Those poor, innocent girls.' She shakes her head. 'Viciously attacked as they walked home from a party. Sixteen years old and left for dead. By some miracle they survived but they haven't been the same since. Rubie was left disfigured...' Marla gestures to the side of her own face. 'And Scarlet, well, she hasn't spoken a word since. Not one according to Silas, their uncle. He moved back permanently to take care of them after their mother passed – God rest her soul – just a few months after the attack. She had MS but Silas swore blind she died of a broken heart after witnessing what happened to her precious girls.'

I scan the article even though Marla barely pauses for breath.

'Such a shame they never found out who was responsible. Of course, the townsfolk had their opinions all right. Consensus was that the Clifton boys – scallywags by all accounts – or the fair workers were to blame, especially as there was another attack the following year in '98, just after we moved here. Let me tell you, I wanted to hightail it right back to Leeds, but my Bruce persuaded me to stay, make a go of family life here as we planned. Thank God we didn't have a daughter is all I can say, or I would have put my foot down.'

'Why did people think these Clifton boys or fair workers were to blame?' I ask. I wasn't expecting to find a local so willing to talk about the town's tragedies this soon, but gossipy Marla is giving me a great head start. Maybe I won't need to stay as long.

'Because the annual Halloween fair was always erected on the land next to Sandy Crest Caravan Park, which was owned by the Cliftons, who took over the place in '97. The boys, Colton and Felton, hung around with the younger fair workers and they made quite the menacing gang at the time.' She shudders. 'I only saw them a couple of times when I was out walking Rye in his pram along the prom – it was the only way he'd settle. Like I say, the sea air worked wonders. Then in '99, we won the petition to get the fair stopped, by which time the Cliftons had already left. That was that. Two attacks, two years running, coinciding with them living here. Draw your own conclusions.' Her already wrinkled forehead concertinas further as she raises her eyebrows.

'But they were never found guilty?' I ask.

'Well, no,' admits Marla. 'They denied it until they were blue in the face by all accounts, and nothing was ever proven, even after the police investigation, but they were pariahs here. And because of the press coverage, Sandy Crest became a ghost town. Seems the general public made up their own minds too. I can't say I blame them, but it was a huge blow to me and my

Bruce straight off the bat. Moving here to run a seaside B&B for holidaymakers that didn't want to come near the place, and after all the travelling back and forth my Bruce did between here and Leeds to view potential properties in the first place. He did end up doing a few cash-in-hand jobs for the Cliftons too, which I won't apologise for – we had a new baby and this place to furnish, and every penny counted! Anyway, all that effort was scuppered just two weeks after we moved in. I mean, one attack is tragic enough but two, and two years running too! We limped on regardless, helped by the fact this was a knockdown price to begin with, but it certainly wasn't the success we hoped it would be.' She sighs wearily.

'And the sisters?' I ask. 'They still don't know who attacked them?'

'Unfortunately not, no.' She pauses, hooks me with her beady gaze. 'I'm surprised you didn't read about it back then if you lived in Leeds. Like I say, we were there till '98 and it was in a few of the Yorkshire papers. Mind you, you're still a spring chicken; it might have passed you by. Anyway, I'll let you get on up to your room and get settled in! What is it you said you did for work again?'

I think it's only fair I reward her with an honest answer for being so unknowingly helpful. She doesn't strike me as the type of woman who would be wary of speaking to a writer. Plus, I'm sure Ebony would have included Delaney Publishing's name on the booking.

'Oh!' she says when I disclose my profession, clearly impressed. 'Like Barbara Cartland? She liked pink too.'

I raise my eyebrows, amused at the comparison. I may have pink hair, but I certainly don't write romance novels. Dark and twisted thrillers are more my style.

'Not exactly,' I tell Marla. 'I'm writing a book series about coastal towns. My client's sent me here for research.'

'How about that!' she says, sounding intrigued. I can almost see her cogs turning, lining up the questions she wants to ask me. But I want to be asking her the questions, not the other way around.

I grab the handle of my wheelie case again. 'Well, I'll go and stash my stuff upstairs.'

'Yes, right you are, dear,' she says, a flash of disappointment crossing her face before she turns down the narrow hallway towards the back of the B&B and a door marked *Private*, dusting the dado rail as she goes.

I slide the copy of the newspaper into my bag and finally head for the stairs, thinking that motormouth landlady Marla may well make my job in this deadbeat town a hell of a lot easier, and the third and final instalment of the *Forgotten Fairground* series might just turn out to be the most interesting of them all.

CHAPTER FOUR

RUBIE

Rubie smacks the side of the ancient printer as it whirrs and clicks ominously. 'For God's sake, please don't jam, please don't jam,' she repeats through gritted teeth, praying to the printer gods. Uncle Silas wouldn't be happy to hear her using God's name in vain, even though he's not exactly devout himself these days. He disappeared earlier and he's still not back. Probably worshipping pints of ale in The Smugglers as usual, thinks Rubie sourly.

'For fuck's sake,' she swears as the printer does jam, its red error light flashing. She sighs and bends forwards, resting her forehead on the edge of the old wooden desk and squeezing her eyes shut. The printer's been on its last legs for ages now, but the thought of having to ask Uncle Silas for money for a new one is too much for her to bear today. He doesn't understand it's a business expense and he'll just complain again about how easily people replace things these days, and how everyone's always chasing the newest technology, and how we live in a throwaway society and don't appreciate the value of money. It's a bit rich coming from the man still living in his late sister's house and off her inheritance, which was – is – supposed to support Rubie and Scarlet as well as maintain the decrepit family homestead with its two acres of land and couple of outbuildings. Instead, he polices every household penny in order to eke the money out for longer, regardless of what his nieces actually need. Yet there always seems to be plenty in his beer fund. If he'd have loosened his iron grip on the purse strings a few years ago, she might have been able to leave this godforsaken house and actually have a life. Put her share of the inheritance towards a house of her own. As it is, she's still here – a thirty-six-year-old woman stuck in time for ever, literally no further on than when she was sixteen. No boyfriend, no husband, no children to bring her happiness and the sense of peace and purpose she craves.

Oak nudges her leg with his snout and she reaches down to stroke his velvet fur, feeling instantly calmer. She looks over at Elm, who is still in her bed in the corner but looking at Rubie inquisitively, her chocolate-brown eyes doleful. Her two working cocker spaniels bring her so much joy and always seem to know when she needs them. She doesn't know what she'll do when she inevitably loses them. They're both eleven now and showing signs of old age, much like herself. They were the reason she started her online business selling organic pet treats and accessories and she still prefers them to people, even her small and loyal customer base. The business only brings in a trickle of income, but it keeps her busy enough. Reduces the ruminating.

'That'll teach me for trying to get ahead for tomorrow,' Rubie says to Oak, smoothing down his long ears. 'I'll have to write the orders by hand in the morning before I go to the post office.' Uncle Silas can't be relied on for any household duties in Rubie's brief absences, so Saturday mornings are her only respite thanks to Dot, their housekeeper, being here to cook, clean and look after Scarlet and the dogs, cats and chickens.

They used to have a horse and rabbits when they were younger, but they're long gone now. She kisses Oak's forehead and stands up, immediately grabbing the edge of the desk as the dizziness causes her to wobble. Even all these years later, she still hates that it's better to move slowly and smoothly. Or maybe just once she wants to outsmart the dizziness, beat it before it happens, stop it happening altogether, somehow. But the doctors made it clear that was unlikely to happen. She closes her eyes and breathes deeply, waiting for it to pass, concentrating on the sound of Oak's tail swishing against the wooden floorboards, of the ticking of the grandfather clock in the hallway, of the beating of her heart in her chest.

After a few minutes the dizziness passes, as it always does, and Rubie abandons the problem printer and heads upstairs. Evening's already setting in, so she flicks the light on as she goes, Oak and Elm bounding up the steps beside her. Dusty frames still adorn the peeling and faded patterned wallpaper alongside lighter patches that show where photographs now long removed once used to hang. Some people don't deserve to be remembered in a family portrait gallery. Rubie rounds the landing and makes her way to the front bedroom. The dogs are already nosing at the door, impatient to get inside.

'Wait,' she tells them as she turns the handle and peeks through the crack. The room is gloomy, but she can make out her sister's sleeping form.

'Go on then.' At their mistress's command, Oak and Elm bustle to the bed, nuzzling Scarlet's arm and hand. She stirs, a smile starting to stretch the corners of her mouth while her eyes remain closed.

'Wakey, wakey, sleepyhead,' sing-songs Rubie, sitting on the edge of the bed and stroking her sister's long dark hair. The dogs, used to the routine, lay at Rubie's feet between the two single beds. The large room is symmetrical; each bed is positioned underneath one of two narrow windows and separated by a dressing table with a small cheval mirror on top. Bedside tables sit on the other sides of the beds and double wardrobes are positioned at the opposite end of the room. A Take That poster is Blu-Tacked to one of the wardrobe doors and holographic stickers are stuck haphazardly around the handles.

Scarlet snaps open her eyes and sits up suddenly, like a Jack-in-the-box. Rubie reaches for the small notebook and pencil from the windowsill behind the curtain and passes them to her sister.

Scarlet takes them and writes on a fresh page of the notebook before showing it to Rubie: *Has he been?*

Rubie smiles sadly at her sister's small but scruffy script. 'No. Father Christmas only comes on Christmas Eve, silly. It's still October.' At the sight of Scarlet's crestfallen expression, Rubie adds, 'But it is our birthday in a few days, so you'll have a present to open then.'

Scarlet claps her hands with glee before posing another question: *How old will we be this year?*

Rubie swallows the lump in her throat, as she does whenever Scarlet asks this. 'Seventeen, of course.'

Scarlet's face lights up. *1 year closer to 18 and leaving this dump for good,* she hurriedly writes next before flinging her arms around Rubie's neck.

Rubie's eyes instantly mist with tears. Sometimes, through Scarlet's scribbled words, she swears she can almost hear her voice and for a split-second she feels like she's got her sister back. Pre-attack Scarlet. Pre-irrevocably damaged Scarlet. Pre-trapped in time Scarlet. A tiny flicker of her old self appears briefly through a teeny tiny crack in her psyche, but then she always disappears into her internal abyss again, sucked back inside herself.

Rubie wishes she had an internal abyss. A safe bubble of alternate reality rather than the memory of that night playing on a loop in her head. It starts up again...

Rubie hears Scarlet scream her name as she stalks out into the misty, drizzly night, walking as fast as she can on her heels, her hair streaming behind her like a thick, glossy ribbon.

'We're going home!' shouts Rubie over her shoulder. She's fizzing with humiliation.

'Wait!' Scarlet manages to catch up to her and grabs her arm. Rubie shakes her off and continues stomping up Kayleigh's driveway. 'Rube!' Scarlet cries.

At the sound of her nickname, Rubie huffs a sigh and turns, crossing her arms and fixing her sister with a stare.

'Why did you leave me? We were meant to stick together. You promised!' Scarlet sticks her bottom lip out like a toddler. It irritates Rubie.

'I was gone for five minutes, Scar! We're not conjoined – I'm allowed to have fun on my own occasionally.'

Scarlet mirrors Rubie's defensive stance. She tilts her head. 'And did you?'

'Did I what?'

'Have fun without me – with Felton?'

Rubie scowls. 'Why, are you jealous?'

'Did you kiss him?' asks Scarlet, stepping closer to Rubie, scrutinising her face.

Rubie can't stop her face from heating, and even in the dim glow from the house she knows Scarlet will notice her flaming cheeks.

'Or didn't he want you?' sneers Scarlet. 'Does he prefer Kayleigh?'

'You're drunk, you lightweight!' snarls Rubie. She wonders

if Scarlet witnessed her tryst in the garden. If she knows exactly what happened and is now enjoying her evident misery. Her sister's head is framed by the full moon. It looks as though she's wearing a halo. Even in her angry state, Rubie can appreciate the irony.

Scarlet laughs and continues her taunts. 'I bet he'd even prefer Rosalie if she was here.'

Rubie's temper erupts. 'Shut up!' she screams in her sister's face. She's had enough. Tonight has been a disaster and she doesn't need her sister rubbing her face in her failure. 'If anyone's going to die a virgin, it's you!'

Scarlet's eyes flash. Instinctively, she lashes out, but Rubie catches her wrist before her palm can make contact with her already flushed cheek. She shoves her sister hard and Scarlet lands on the paved driveway with a squeal.

'Say sorry, you little bitch!' demands Rubie, hands on hips, staring down at Scarlet.

Scarlet glares back, teeth gritted, nostrils flaring. Rubie waits. 'Sorry,' she says eventually, looking away first to inspect her grazed palms.

Rubie sighs and drops her shoulders. She nods once. 'Now get up. Like I said before, we're going home.'

'How?' asks Scarlet, pushing herself up and massaging her wrists.

'How do you think?'

'It's too dark!' Scarlet protests. 'And we can't walk by ourselves. Uncle Silas says it's not safe during fair week.'

Rubie raises her eyebrows. 'Do you think it's any safer hitching a lift?'

After barely a moment's deliberation, Scarlet shakes her head.

'Exactly. Now hurry the fuck up!' Rubie commands as she wraps her arms around her slim frame.

Scarlet scurries after her sister. Ballet pumps long forgotten and still wedged under the hedge, they link arms and wobble down the long driveway on their heels and out onto the dark, deserted road...

Rubie can never escape the ever-present memory but returns Scarlet's embrace, hugging her skinny body tightly. 'How about we bake ourselves a cake this year? I'll go and get the ingredients tomorrow after I've been to the post office.'

Scarlet pulls back, eyes wide and excited. *Chocolate cake* she writes.

'Chocolate cake,' confirms Rubie as Scarlet claps her hands, causing the dogs to rise. 'Come on, let's go downstairs and get something to eat. There's plenty of Dot's batch cooking left in the freezer.'

As she stands, ready to help Scarlet up after her afternoon nap, Rubie catches sight of her reflection in the dressing-table mirror and instantly averts her eyes from the grotesqueness she perceives. Even now, twenty years later, she still desperately misses the dewy-skinned, pouty-lipped, naturally beautiful teenager she once was. She still hasn't come to terms with being this haggard, disfigured, almost middle-aged husk of a woman wearing her dead mother's old clothes, and she knows she never will. She's not sure if she can actually remember being bludgeoned that night, or whether her nightmares have cruelly filled in the big, black blank of the attack with their own realistic, Technicolour re-enactment, forcing her to relive it again and again. Sometimes it's as though she's watching it on screen, removed from herself, as her eye socket explodes and her jaw fractures, and she's aghast anew at the utter horror of it. But even that doesn't compare to the first time she saw her reflection afterwards. She was never as bookish as Rosie but even Rubie doubts Mary Shelley's description of Frankenstein's monster was as horrific as what she saw in the mirror that day.

Scarlet reaches for Rubie's hand as they follow the dogs along the landing and then the sisters steadily descend the stairs, Scarlet clutching the banister on one side and Rubie on the other.

'Do you need your wheelchair?' Rubie asks her as they reach the bottom step. One of the cats slink by and they wait for it to pass.

Scarlet shakes her head but grips Rubie a little bit tighter as they slowly cross the flagstone floor into the kitchen, their bodies pressed together as though they are joined at the hips. Rubie supposes they are, to all intents and purposes. Practically conjoined twins, despite what she spitefully retorted that night. If they weren't so tragic, they'd be considered pathetic, still living together in their childhood home, sharing their childhood bedroom, merely existing. Rubie feels as though she has been sleepwalking for the past twenty years, struggling to make sense of what happened to them or to move on from it. Sometimes she envies Scarlet her amnesia, her ignorance, her confusion about what day or month or year it is. Rubie's face may be split and cracked and scarred, but her brain is annoyingly sharp. Except for two unanswered questions that plague her constantly: who did this to them and why?

Dad's dead!!! I can't believe I'm even writing this. It feels like a bad dream. He died on Friday, two days ago, but it already feels like he's been gone forever. He was riding Maple on the bridle path near the beach. Uncle Silas found him and said she either threw him off or he fell off. We don't know for sure. Something must have scared her because she's not a skittish horse. Uncle Silas said Dad was already dead before the ambulance even got there. The paramedics said he had severe head and neck injuries and was bleeding inside himself. I keep thinking of him just lying there on his own waiting for someone to help him and I can't make the thought go away! If Uncle Silas hadn't been visiting and gone looking for him, how long would it have been before he was found? Why couldn't someone have saved him in time?

Maple's back in the barn now. I tried to go out there yesterday, but I couldn't bring myself to. None of us can even look at her. I know it's not really her fault but why is she still alive and Dad's not? Uncle Silas says he'll take care of her if that's what Mum wants, but it didn't sound like he meant he'd look after her.

I don't know what's going to happen to us all now, especially as Mum's been so poorly lately. She always needs to lie down and hates our music being on loud and gets really upset when the three of us argue. She doesn't even like watching TV because her eyes hurt. I snuck down for a drink last night and I heard her crying. It was so awful. She was asking Uncle Silas to promise to help take care of us if she gets worse, and then they prayed together, like that ever works! I haven't told Rubie or Rosalie yet because that will make it more real. None of us want him here even now and I don't want anything to happen to Mum either. Everything is awful!

FRIDAY 27TH OCTOBER 2017

CHAPTER FIVE

ALLIE

I pass two closed doors on the first-floor landing before I reach the door leading into the room at the front of the property. It's ajar and bears a screwed-on number one. I push it open fully and yank my wheelie case in behind me. The décor in here very much mirrors downstairs: a thick candlewick bedspread and heavy textured curtains framing the large bay window. But it's clean and cosy and fine for a few days. Being in a place like this reminds me of impromptu summer weekends away with Claudia. We'd just take off after she finished work on a Friday evening and "follow the bonnet", as she'd say, to wherever took our fancy. Usually Filey or Saltburn or Cayton Bay. We'd ask the neighbour to feed Story and off we'd go, giddy and giggling, feeling frivolous and so in love.

The scenes swirl around my brain before steadily settling, solid and suffocating. The familiar sadness soaks into my heart and I realise I need a dose of fresh air. I want a stiff sea breeze to blow the memories away before I can gather them any closer and marinate in them, becoming even more maudlin than I already am. Failing that, I'll have to find a temporary distraction to keep them at arm's length, at least for the rest of the night.

I unzip my wheelie case to get my jacket and then leave the room, locking the door behind me. Thankfully, Marla's nowhere to be seen as I exit the B&B, but I still dart out the main door just in case she's lurking and hankering to chat again. As useful as she might be to me, I'm not in the mood for more history right now. I scurry across the road then slow my steps as I reach the prom.

Aside from a jogger up ahead and a dog energetically frolicking around its owner on the beach, I'm virtually alone as I head towards the pier, which looks like a derelict building on rotting stilts. There are no fancy art deco lampposts or countless strings of coloured bulbs here like you might find in a livelier seaside town, but the few streetlights from the higher main road to my left cast a sufficient glow as I stroll towards nowhere.

Underfoot, the prom's paving is cracked and all that separates it from the beach below are rusted iron railings, a few of which are missing completely. I take out my phone and snap a few pictures. They won't be good enough quality to put in Ralph's book, but they'll come in handy if I need to pad scenic descriptions out accurately, however run-down and unappealing they are. Not that I want a personal reminder of this view but I'm all for anything that makes my life easier down the line. It's all just fucking depressing though – the neglected surroundings and the tragic history of the place. It's like a stereotypical abandoned town in a low-budget movie. I'm half expecting a horde of zombies to appear any moment. At his point, I might not even bother running from them. The wind picks up and I zip my jacket up tighter. God, I need a drink.

As if my prayer was heard for once, I round the bend and immediately spy a pub across the road. Its wooden sign creaks in the breeze bearing the name *The Smugglers Arms*. The warmth of its lounge is pleasant, and the barmaid hands me my requested glass of red wine with practised efficiency, minimal chitchat, and no judgy glance at my hair. Just how I like it. I choose to sit at a small round table near one of the mullioned windows, savouring my first sip of the smooth alcohol as I listen to snatches of conversations and avoid eye contact with anyone.

Once settled in, I surreptitiously scope the bar for someone to potentially have a bit of fun with. It's slim pickings though – a handful of haggard older couples barely interacting, a few middle-aged, rosy-nosed, lone men supping cloudy pints of ale, and a group of three twenty-somethings drinking Cokes and playing cards, who are all far too young for me. I should have known better; small towns like this never change. Feeling the faint twinge of frustration, I resort to opening the dating app I've recently reinstalled on my phone. I log in but the familiar name and fonts and icons and photos only stir up old feelings and compound my loneliness. Nonetheless, I change the search criteria to men only for fear of seeing Claudia's profile back online (or her sister Shelley's – God forbid) and begin to swipe half-heartedly. None of them spark my interest.

A short while later, as I'm about to drain my glass and leave, a young, ginger-haired kid holding an almost full pint approaches my table. He's probably a third of the age of most of the other men in here but most definitely not my type. Where men are concerned, I like mine more mature, in every sense. Women too. Claudia had a few years on me but unfortunately, her biological clock reminded her of that often. And in turn, she reminded me, time and time again. Gentle persuasion morphed into tearful ultimatums and then into silent resentment. She wanted us to have a child together and I didn't want to have a child full stop. Stalemate. Heartbreak.

'Anyone sitting here?' the kid asks me, gesturing to the stool opposite.

'The Invisible Man,' I reply sardonically. I don't want to waste my evening on an unsuitable prospect.

He laughs and reaches for the stool, tipping it up. 'Oops, sorry, mate,' he says before sitting down on it. 'Seems the Invisible Man has disappeared.' He laughs again at his own joke, and I try my best to disguise my amusement, but it tickled me. Still, he's too young.

'Not seen you around here before,' he states.

'Wow. What an original observation,' I say.

He smiles widely, showing off even teeth, the front two ever so slightly crossed. He's got a smattering of freckles across his nose and cheeks, which complement his hair. He's not a bad-looking boy but he has a vague look of someone I once knew, someone I don't want to be reminded of. Another strike against him. 'Practically everyone in Stonethorpe is my mum's age or older. It's rare to see someone else with barely any wrinkles.'

His cheeky comment surprises me and makes me laugh despite myself. Not least because the fact I barely have any wrinkles is down to my regular Botox and filler injections and not just my age or genetics. It's amazing what regular liquid-filled needles wielded by an expert can do. Still, I appreciate the compliment, so I close the dating app and set my phone down on the table, willing to interact with him after all.

'Have you lived here your whole life?' I ask, thawing my tone slightly. Folding my jacket over my lap, I take another small sip of my drink. Even chatting with a kid is better than being alone at the B&B torturing myself about what, or who, Claudia might be doing now, I suppose.

He nods. 'Since I was a baby. I can't wait to leave though. Move to London and join the police. Nothing happens here, nothing since the attacks anyway. It's so boring.'

I raise my eyebrows. 'Get off on violent crimes, do you?'

He raises his hands, palms facing me, a panicked look in his eyes like a suspect caught red-handed. 'No, nothing like that! I just mean… you know… living here is like repeating the same mundane *Groundhog Day* over and over and over.'

I study him for a few seconds, remembering the intoxicating feeling all too well. The longing for change, for adventure. But life often has a cruel way of misinterpreting that yearning. 'Be careful what you wish for,' I warn him. 'Excitement can be overrated.'

'Not if you've never had any,' he counters after swallowing a mouthful of his drink. 'My dad died last year and my mum needs help, but I can't just stay here forever working in a café, seeing the same old faces day in and day out. I feel like I'm missing out.'

'Sorry about your dad,' I reply. 'It's tough losing a parent. I know what you mean about small towns though. I'd hate living here too.' I finish my glass of wine and briefly consider getting another when a deep, raspy Scottish voice punctuates the quiet hum of the pub, drawing every gaze to its owner.

The kid swivels towards the noise too, and we both watch an old, tall, grey-bearded man leaning sloppily against the bar, repeating his slurred request for a pint.

The indifferent barmaid stubbornly ignores him and moves briskly towards another customer, her lips pursed with irritation, at the same time as an older man, presumably the landlord, appears from the back of the bar. His broad shoulders are stooped and rounded; no doubt due to the weight of dealing with inebriated characters like this one.

'Go back home, Silas,' he says with a predictably weary tone. 'You've already had enough by the looks of it.'

'I've not had nearly enough, man!' the bearded man states loudly.

The landlord crosses his arms and shakes his head to reinforce his refusal to serve another drink.

The kid turns back to me and thumbs at the scene behind

him. 'That's Silas Sanderson,' he whispers. 'Resident drunk and loudmouth.'

Before I can respond, Silas slaps his large hand down on the top of the bar and the barmaid jumps. 'C'mon, Keith, you know what week it is.'

The landlord sighs before rounding the front of the bar. He reaches Silas, holding one hand out and gesturing with his other, presumably in an attempt to prevent a bigger scene and shepherd him outside. Already I doubt he'll succeed – I've seen men like Silas before.

'C'mon, man!' Silas shouts again, stepping back, proving me right. He wobbles and leans back against the bar. 'I just want a drink in my local boozer. I've every right to drown my sorrows, y'know.' He points around the pub at nobody in particular. Some avert their eyes, some roll their eyes, some openly stare and nudge each other, clearly enjoying the spectacle. 'Twenty years!' Silas roars, spittle visibly flying from his mouth. 'Twenty years this week and look at us all! As pathetic now as we were then. If it hadn't have happened, I wouldn't even be here in this godforsaken town, and neither would my wee nieces. We'd all be thriving, and so would you...' He sweeps an arm wide, and Keith the landlord swerves back to avoid being caught in its loose arc. 'That fucking fair... those evil Cliftons... and all you lot did was shut the gate after the horses had already bolted and trampled over—' He stops abruptly as his wild, bloodshot gaze falls upon me. 'And look! Look!'

Silas slams his hand down again for emphasis then lurches forwards as though about to make a beeline for me. Keith immediately forms a barrier with his arm and speaks quietly to him. Whatever warning words he's uttering clearly fall on deaf ears as Silas jabs a dirty, long-nailed finger in my direction. I'm surprised he can even focus in his state. I clock the kid shifting subtly to shield me from the old man's direct view and I'm grateful for the gesture.

'You're still letting outsiders walk freely among us,' says Silas, before turning up the volume even more to address the whole pub. 'And with fucking pink hair!' He snorts, a disgusting phlegmy sound, before continuing his tirade, '"Beware of false prophets, who come to you in sheep's clothing but inwardly are ravenous wolves!" Have you learnt nothing?'

'Want to get out of here?' the kid whispers across the table as Silas continues to rant, throwing up his arms whenever Keith again attempts to steer him towards the door. 'There's another exit out the back.' He points to a narrow corridor to the side of the bar.

'We can only trust our own!' booms Silas, his words laced with vitriol. Behind him, the barmaid wears a bored expression while the other patrons keep their heads and eyes down, unwilling to get involved.

'I'll find it myself,' I say to the kid, slipping my phone in my pocket and clutching my coat and bag before standing and hurrying out without even saying goodbye. I exit out of an external door onto a small, brick-walled yard and weave my way between three sets of wooden tables and chairs to get back onto the street. Pausing for a moment to catch my breath and get my bearings, I pull my coat on, turn left and head back to the B&B alone.

The entrance hall is again Marla-free and I hurry straight upstairs to my room. I'm not in the habit of letting crazy old codgers spook me but the whole scene in the pub definitely dampened my need for company of any kind, and I'd rather just get an early night now.

After changing into one of Claudia's old T-shirts to sleep in, which I stole before Shelley descended, I open my laptop to review and add to my notes on the shared Google Docs files with all the information I've found out from Marla and the kid so far. The last thing I want is another phone call from Ebony chasing me for an update. I then double-check what time I'm meeting with Mason McKenzie in the morning. Ralph has obviously pulled some strings by lining up the award-winning retired journalist to provide accurate historic context for the book. Or maybe Ebony arranged it directly. She's a terrier and doesn't let up until she gets a yes. I take another look at the front-page news story that she sent over earlier, written by the man himself:

Seaside Town Shut Down Annual Fair
After Repeated Violent Crimes

May 1999
By Mason McKenzie

Stonethorpe-On-Sea residents are rejoicing this week after winning an injunction preventing the travelling community from bringing the annual Halloween fair to town. Maeve Hodgeson, the town's postmistress, instigated a petition against the travelling "fun" fair and its workers after the brutal attack on Rubie and Scarlet Sanderson in October 1997 and a sexual assault on a young woman who wishes to remain anonymous in October 1998. Both serious crimes occurred during "fair week".

The Sanderson sisters were callously left for dead whilst walking home from a local house party just days before their seventeenth birthday. Scarlet, now dubbed "the silent sister" as she has not spoken a word since, not only sustained serious wounds from the attack itself but was further injured when she was knocked down in a hit-and-run when bravely trying to flag down help for herself and Rubie. The young women have remained dependents of their uncle, Silas Sanderson, in their erstwhile family home, since returning from hospital several weeks after the violent incident. Sadly, prior to their return, their chronically ill mother passed away. A Stonethorpe native, Mr Sanderson moved back to town from Scotland permanently to take care of his nieces following the death of his sister. He declared the attacks "pure evil".

Despite extensive local police investigations, no attacker has yet been brought to justice for any of the assaults on the three women, although police still believe the attacks are related.

North East Lincolnshire council finally awarded the injunction after months of deliberation.

Ms Hodgeson stated, 'Community safety takes priority over the additional tourism the fair brought to our town. We are heartened that the council are committed to ensuring travelling fair workers cannot descend upon us and commit further heinous crimes in Stonethorpe-On-Sea. We look forward to rebuilding our reputation as a safe seaside town in the years to come.'

I notice there's no mention of the speculation about the Cliftons that Marla spoke of and make a mental note to ask Mason why he didn't include that in the article if rumours were so rife. Maybe he didn't need to if the witch hunt was already in full formation. Perhaps he included it in earlier or later articles instead. Either way, I'm sure I'll find out tomorrow.

As I'm drifting off to sleep, a series of creaks brings me back to full consciousness. I sit up and look towards the door. A strip of light underlines it from the illuminated landing. I hold my breath to hear better and a few seconds later I recognise the sound of a nearby door clicking shut. My heartbeat quickens; I thought I was the only guest staying here. Throwing back the duvet and the candlewick bedspread, I slip out of bed to retrieve the can of rape spray from my bag. I get back in bed and slide it under my pillow. The kid in the pub might have described Stonethorpe-On-Sea as practically comatose, but in my experience, you can never be too careful.

CHAPTER SIX

RUBIE

Rubie's favourite moment is the exquisite limbo between sleeping and waking. In those few seconds, she's still sixteen years old, with her whole life ahead of her. In her dreams, Felton Clifton is besotted with her. He's the older bad boy who was tamed by the sweet but hot virginal girl, who didn't remain a virgin for long once she'd agreed to be his girlfriend, officially. In Rubie's fantasies, she and Felton parade around the Halloween fair just days after she finally caught his eye at Kayleigh's party, his protective and possessive arm slung around her slender shoulders as Kayleigh and the other popular girls scowl with narrowed eyes, seething with jealousy.

She feels smug in the dream, and proud, as she slides her hand into the back pocket of his jeans and his thumb strokes her soft and, as yet, unblemished and unscarred cheek. They're young, they're gorgeous, they're Johnny Depp and Winona Ryder before the split, but they're going to last because Felton adores her, and she idolises him. They'll move to a bustling city and live rock star lifestyles in a house with a Gothic façade, and their children will be beautiful with cool and unique names. Or they'll live a slower-paced existence in a quaint countryside cottage with a stream at the bottom of the mature garden, the soothing trickle a pleasant accompaniment to the lawn games and family picnics every summer.

Rubie wakes with a jolt, one palm flat against her scar as it often is, as though concealing it even from her unconscious self. She runs her fingertips along its seams and over the tighter, thinner skin that was grafted on from her forehead. The texture of it repulses her. She checks the time and sees it's just before midnight. She's only been asleep for an hour. She screws her eyes back shut, desperate to freefall back to the vividness of the delicious dream, to sink into the pretence again, but she can already sense something is not as it should be.

Opening her eyes reluctantly, she turns to face her sister in their shared room. She's lost count of the number of times she's found Scarlet staring back at her, a wide-eyed haunted look on her face. Or huddled in her duvet on the floor, sucking strands of her hair in her sleep. But tonight, by the glow of Scarlet's nightlight, Rubie only sees an empty single bed. She can hear the gentle purr of one of the cats and suspects it has made a cosy nest within Scarlet's discarded bedding.

Easing herself up and shrugging on her dressing gown, Rubie tiptoes downstairs, careful not to make any sounds that might disturb her uncle. She didn't hear him come home but it's not unusual for him to be crashed out on the living-room sofa in a drunken slumber, his deep, guttural snores often reverberating around the house. She can't hear him tonight but if he is asleep, the last thing Rubie wants is to wake him up.

The kitchen floor's flagstones are cold under her bare feet, but the old Aga wedged beneath the tall, wide fireplace ensures the large room itself stays warm enough despite Uncle Silas's tight-fisted approach to supposed "luxuries" such as certain foods, heat and hot water. As Rubie creeps past the central pine table, Oak raises his head and Elm follows suit, but they don't move from their beds beside the Aga. Rubie can already see why: Scarlet is also curled up in Elm's bed. Conflicting feelings pang inside her: pride that Scarlet made it all the way downstairs by herself and sympathy for her permanently childlike thirty-six-year-old sister, but most predominantly, she feels pity.

Rubie remembers how pale and pathetic Scarlet looked in her hospital bed after their attack, when she was finally taken to see her. After the horror of waking up in an alternate reality, bandaged and broken, hearing but not listening to softly spoken doctors and nurses, pain pulsing through her like electric shocks, her first thought wasn't for herself but for her sister, who for once wasn't in the bed next to her. Scarlet didn't wake from her coma until nine weeks afterwards, and in that time, their mum had taken a turn for the worse too. At the time, Rubie assumed the rapid decline was due to the stress of her beloved girls' near-death experience, which was bad enough, but she's often wondered since if Rosie's selfish disappearance, precisely when their mum needed her other strong, sensible daughter the most, caused the most damage. Especially as she then had no choice but to ask Silas to come home to Stonethorpe-On-Sea, which only made things harder for them all.

Rubie gently sweeps Scarlet's curtain of long black hair away from her face and strokes the damp strands all the way to the ends until Scarlet stirs. 'Hello, sleepyhead.' She smiles as Scarlet opens her eyes. 'Shall we go back to our own beds?'

Rubie manages to tug Scarlet to her feet and taking steady steps as usual, they navigate their way to the staircase, Scarlet's head resting on Rubie's shoulder. As they begin their ascent, Elm bunny-hops ahead of them but the sound of Oak's nails tip-tapping on the floor stops and is replaced by a low growl.

'Oak, what is—'

Before Rubie can even finish asking the question, the

pounding on the front door makes them both jump and Oak's growl becomes a protective bark.

'Girls!' Silas shouts in his deep Scottish burr. 'I forgot my key. C'mon now and let your old uncle in!'

Rubie rolls her eyes, in annoyance and frustration. She thought the house was too quiet; she should have known he'd grace them with his drunken presence at the worst possible moment. 'Pretty please... with a cherry on top.' His manic laugh segues into a hiccup, and he hammers a few more times on the door for good measure. 'Rubie, I know you can hear me, my girl!'

Rather than attempt to hurry Scarlet upstairs while enduring Silas's slurred demands, Rubie helps her to sit down on a step then goes back down to open the door. Oak still hasn't stopped barking. Silas may be master of the house now but dogs sense danger no matter what.

Rubie opens up and stands back to let her uncle shuffle into the house, restraining Oak by his collar.

'Guess what I found out from Keith? Y'know... Keith at The Smugglers?' he asks without preamble as he stops in the centre of the large square hallway, swaying slightly.

Rubie instructs Oak to stay and returns to Scarlet, who is clutching the stair spindles and watching Silas warily.

'Well, there's a writer in our midst. The rumour is she's poking her nose into our story.' He pokes at his own nose and misses. 'Twenty years too late though, isn't she?' He cackles.

'Our story, not yours,' retorts Rubie.

'What's that now, my girl?' shouts Silas, stepping forward and clutching a spindle. Scarlet recoils into Rubie, turning her face away from their uncle. 'So the fact that I slef... slef...' – he pauses, clearly trying to connect his addled brain to his slackened mouth but doesn't manage to – '...sleflessly returned to my childhood home to take care of you two orphan Annies doesn't feature in the story, is that it?'

'You don't take care of us, not really, and nobody's making you stay here!' says Rubie, emboldened by her anger.

He snorts derisively but his eyes are full of spite. 'As if you wee girlies could cope on your own. Social services would split you up like that.' He tries to click his fingers, but they just slide against each other ineffectually.

'Don't pretend you're holier than thou. For a so-called man of God, you're only here for yourself.'

'Maself? You think this is the life I wanted – raising my dead sister's brats in Shithorpe-On-Sea?' He holds out his hands and shrugs, an exaggerated gesture combined with an exaggerated expression, wet mouth downturned, beady eyes widened.

'Raising?' Rubie asks, the word loaded with contempt. 'Apart from occasional visits when we were kids, you weren't interested in us. The only reason you stayed after Mum died was because you wanted the respect and adoration that came with being the town's hero. But nobody respects or adores the local drunk!'

'And who drove me to drink, girl?' Silas snarls.

'Don't you dare try and blame us. We needed help... we needed you, but you let us down. You should be ashamed of yourself. What would Reverend Kiely say if I told him what you're really like?'

Silas bares his discoloured teeth at Rubie and Oak stands to attention again. 'If I find out you've said a word to the vicar, I'll make sure you pay, lassie. And I'll know it was you because it's not as if this one is going to say anything, is it?' He nods at Scarlet and sneers, seeming more sober now. 'All this came about because two randy harlots snuck out to a party and ran into trouble. God knew you two girls were wicked, so he taught you a lesson.' Spittle dots his lips as he speaks, and Rubie feels the usual hatred swell within her. She despises this disgusting man with every fibre of her being. No matter how many times they have a version of this argument, he always manages to find a way to inject even more poison. She stares him dead in the eyes while willing herself not to cry.

'Well, he must have punished you for your sins, too, because now we're all in hell,' she says through gritted teeth.

She drags Scarlet up and they make it up the rest of the stairs and back to their bedroom, all the while accompanied by the background track of Silas's shouted stream of religious passages as he lurches into the kitchen, no doubt in search of a nightcap to tip him over into oblivion.

As Rubie tucks Scarlet back into bed, she finally lets her tears spill over. After kissing her sister's forehead, she crosses the room to lock the door, swerving around the dogs now settled on the rug. Guilt thrums within her. She knows that given half the chance, she'd leave here too. She hates acknowledging it to herself, but she and Silas have one thing in common: they're both martyrs. Staying because it's the "right" thing to do. She loves Scarlet, she really does, but she's resentful too. She's trapped here, in this tiny town, as her sister's carer, with a drunken uncle who detests them. And there's absolutely nothing she can do about it. Is there?

SATURDAY 28TH OCTOBER 2017

CHAPTER SEVEN

FENIX

The old staircase creaks under Fenix's careful steps as he descends to the main hallway. He can detect the faint aroma of fried bacon and hear the hum of a radio playing tinny music. Rather than making him feel hungry, the food smell churns his stomach.

'Good morning, dear. I thought I heard someone coming down. Sleep well?' Marla asks, appearing as if by magic through the dining-room doorway as he reaches the bottom of the stairs. She's wearing a faded floral pinny over her skirt, blouse and cardigan and drying her hands on a checked tea towel. Her manner emits warmth, even for a guest she only met hours ago.

Fenix smiles at her with practised ease, hoping it's enough to draw attention away from the dark bags under his eyes. His insomnia is getting worse. 'Morning. Yes, thanks. Sorry again for turning up so late last night,' he says. 'It's good of you to accommodate me a night earlier than originally planned.'

She flicks his apology away with the tea towel before tucking it into her waistband. 'No bother at all. Occasional late nights are one of the very few drawbacks of being a landlady.

I've just made a start on breakfast, and you're welcome to wait in the dining room until it's served at 8am.'

'Thank you,' he replies, hooking his cross-body bag over his head and pulling his jacket collar up. 'But I'm feeling a bit under the weather, so I thought I'd go for a bracing walk along the seafront. I find fresh air often works wonders first thing.'

'Oh,' says Marla, her sparse but dark brows knitting together above kind eyes. 'I'm sorry to hear you're not feeling well but I'll take your word for it about the fresh air, dear. It's looking a bit grim out there today. Not sure it'll lift anyone's spirits.'

Fenix glances towards the large wooden front door as the brisk wind rattles its stained-glass panes.

'You'd be surprised,' he says.

'Can I offer you a piece of fruit or a slice of toast before you go if you don't fancy something cooked?' she asks.

Fenix presses his palms together in a gesture of gratitude and points them towards Marla. 'You're very thoughtful but no, thank you. I'll just have to wait for the queasiness to subside.'

She eyes him closely, a maternal concern radiating from her. 'Well, if you're sure? I don't like the thought of a strapping young man going about his day on an empty stomach.'

Fenix laughs. 'I appreciate both compliments even though I'm neither strapping nor young anymore,' he says, gesturing to himself, knowing that underneath his layered clothes his once strong, lean body is withering away at an alarming speed. 'And as much as false perceptions can sustain us temporarily, I prefer to face reality these days.'

'Well, good for you,' says Marla, although her gaze remains sympathetic. 'I must admit, I'm often away with the fairies myself. My Bruce used to say I lived in a fantasy land, always hoping for the best and seeing the good in people and situations.'

'If that's your outlook, you'd make a good counsellor,' Fenix remarks with a smile.

'Is that what you do, dear – counselling?' she asks, sharp on the uptake, her curiosity genuine.

His smile evaporates. 'I used to, yes.'

She squints slightly, as though reading between the lines of his answer and deliberating whether or not to dig deeper. He is relieved when she doesn't.

'Good on you for helping people. I've never given a thought to doing anything besides running this place and raising my son for the past twenty years. That's plenty to be getting on with for me. Best job in the world being a parent. Have you got any little ones?'

This is a question he welcomes. He nods, the usual warmth flickering in his chest whenever he thinks of her. 'Just the one. A little girl.'

'How precious,' says Marla, her voice faintly edged with longing. 'Such a shame you didn't bring her with you, dear. Children always benefit from a bit of sea air. It's one of the reasons me and my Bruce chose to raise our boy here.'

Fenix smiles again, a visual platitude. He's had enough of small talk now. 'Maybe next time. Anyway, I must let you get on.'

Marla snaps her gaze to the grandfather clock nearby and flaps her tea towel again as a show of her industriousness. 'Yes indeed, would you look at the time! Breakfast won't cook itself if I'm standing here gabbing! Are you sure I can't even tempt you with a bacon sandwich?'

'I'm sure,' he says firmly but politely.

'Well, enjoy your walk. Do you need directions anywhere?' She doesn't wait for a response before adding, 'My son works at the caff about a mile down the road if you do get a bit peckish later. It's halfway between here and Sandy Crest...' She tuts and shakes her head. 'Ignore me, dear. Us locals still call it Sandy Crest, but that caravan park is long gone, and good riddance to it.'

Fenix frowns at the remark but doesn't press it despite Marla's perhaps deliberate pause. 'Anyway,' she continues, 'you won't miss the caff if you just take a right and keep walking along the prom. Tell them I sent you – they might even give you a discount on a cuppa and a pastry.'

'I wouldn't dream of it. I'm happy to pay full price,' he says.

'Well, that's very honourable of you, dear.' She stretches her thin, painted lips into a smile, which lingers for a moment before she pivots towards the dining room, her movements purposeful once again. 'Right then, my other guest will be down any minute, so I'd better hotfoot it back to the kitchen. Mind how you go now.'

Fenix briefly raises a hand as Marla bustles off down the corridor, then he makes his way to the front door thinking about the word she just used to describe him: honourable. Not yet he isn't, not really, but he hopes to be by the end of this trip. He has spent his whole counselling career attempting to atone, to achieve that elusive state of self-actualisation where his actions are congruent with the perception of himself. There's a phrase he frequently recalls from his training: *it's rarely the present moment causing you pain.* But he is in pain, in all sorts of ways, there's no doubt about that, and he knows from all the victims and troubled souls he's counselled over the years that the aftershocks of trauma linger far into the future, like a noxious gas. The undisputable fact is that he was the one who caused another human's pain in his past life and now that his own future is limited, he wants to subdue those aftershocks for one person in particular more than anything, before it's too late.

The chill from outside seeps straight through the narrow gap at the bottom of the B&B's threshold and he pulls his beanie hat over his stubbled head. Reaching into his bag, he pulls out his wallet and flips it open. He's already smiling, genuinely this time, consciously appreciating the joy he always feels when gazing at the photo of Janelle and Milly. It's his favourite picture from Milly's most recent birthday, just after she lost her second front baby tooth. Her tongue is poking through her double-gapped grin and Janelle is gazing at her rather than the camera, her intense love for their daughter evident on her face.

He's so lucky to have them, to have a family of his own, to have Janelle's total acceptance of not only the imperfect man he is now but the wayward man he once was. She's stuck by him all this time and he's worked hard to be deserving of such a steadfast and compassionate woman. His life could have so easily taken a very dark turn down a very different path. But now he wants to ask for forgiveness for the abhorrent crime he committed, for the justice he evaded, all those years ago, and he knows that the best place to start is here. He returns his wallet to the safety of his bag and opens the door. The sound of waves thrashing greets him as he steps outside, an apt soundtrack to his fierce sense of determination. It's time to seek closure.

CHAPTER EIGHT

ALLIE

I step out of the compact shower cubicle in the B&B's en suite and catch sight of my opaque outline in the steamed-up mirror, which is screwed into the retro aquamarine tiles above the vanity unit opposite. Steam curls like ghostly breath in the enclosed space and I sweep a palm over the surface of the glass, bringing my reflection into view. Reaching for a towel, I blot my face dry, the slightly tatty but clean-smelling cotton noticeably scratchy against my sensitive skin.

The lighting here is much harsher than at home due to there being no window, and the bald patches in my thin, chin-length wet hair are even more prominent than I thought. I've got so used to seeing myself in carefully positioned mirrors or wigs that I'm both surprised and revolted. Sighing with annoyance, I grab my comb and quickly rake it through the strands, before teasing and smoothing them with my fingers, covering up the patches as best as I can.

Before I begin my usual skincare routine, I lean closer to the mirror to scrutinise my face. Every tiny wrinkle, every enlarged pore stands out on my pale skin under the fluorescent light.

After a few moments of close assessment, I decide I need both Botox and filler top-ups, as well as tanning drops. I'll probably order another new wig soon, too, as the alopecia isn't showing any signs of slowing its rampage on my scalp. These minor interventions have become something of a ritual – just enough to smooth over the cracks and enhance my true self. Dropping the towel from my body, I stare critically at my shoulders, breasts and torso, before putting my gold chain back on, resting its locket flat against my jugular notch. Not bad, I conclude, considering I'm knocking on forty.

I lean closer to the mirror and run my hand over my neck and down my body, appraising my skin closely and then as I reach my lower abdomen, I trace the old horizontal scar tissue with my finger. I look down at it, the usual intrusive thoughts running through my head, but snap my head up when I hear the phone ringing in the bedroom. Thankful for the distraction, I wrap the towel back around myself and leave the en suite to answer the call. I'm marginally relieved to see it's Ralph's name rather than Ebony's on the screen.

'What's up, Ralph?' I ask. We dispensed with the mundane pleasantries a while ago; neither of us can stand unnecessary waffle.

'Morning, Allie.' He sighs heavily and I immediately tense. I can already sense the extra pressure he's going to pile on me off the back of the shared files I updated last night. It often feels like a curse being thorough at my job even though I know it'll lead to more work. I wish I was one of those people who can scrape by doing the bare minimum without giving a fuck what anyone else thinks of them, but I'm not. In fact, I probably care *too* much what other people think of me, especially fellow professionals in the industry who I respect, like Ralph. The fact that he's ringing me himself rather than delegating the task to Ebony means he's either stressed or hyped up, so I'm primed for the knock-on effect that's going to have on my day.

'Ebony forwarded me the latest sales figures for the *Forgotten Fairground* series so far last night and although they're healthy enough, I definitely think we need to make this new instalment a bit... juicier, shall we say, than the other books. No point sending my number one ghostwriter on a comped research trip if we don't wring every last penny out of it, is there?' He laughs his breathy, insincere laugh and I don't respond. He knows I'm not the laugh-along type. 'Anyway,' he powers on, more forthright now, 'this interview with Mason McKenzie – get whatever you can from him. Quiz him about this Sanderson sisters' business as a priority. You might be able to dig up fresh dirt, what with it being the twentieth anniversary of their attack, and he knows more about the story than anyone.'

'Fresh dirt? How oxymoronic,' I say, sitting down on the end of the bed, my fingers finding their way to the biggest bald patch on my head. I can't help it; it's like picking at a crusty scab or poking a tongue in an empty tooth socket. I stare ahead absent-mindedly. The curtains are open a crack and a slice of concrete-coloured sea is just visible beyond.

'You know what I mean, Allie. And perhaps save the big words for the book.'

I roll my eyes. Ralph can be snide at times. But so can I. 'Sure. Let's piggyback on an ancient tragedy to sell more books. It's worked for newspapers for decades.'

'Exactly my point,' he replies, choosing to sidestep my sarcastic tone. 'Which Mason McKenzie knows only too well too.' At least he's being honest.

Frowning, I try a different tack. 'From what I've read and heard so far, the attack on those sisters had nothing to do with the Halloween fair itself, so how is it even relevant in a book series about fairgrounds?'

'Because the fair, the town and the attack are all linked, Allie. The fair may not have been a permanent fixture, but it was an annual event that boosted Stonethorpe-On-Sea's infrastructure and brought in tourists from far and wide, as well as the fair workers themselves. And they were prime suspects in the attack, were they not?'

I shrug even though he can't see me. 'Apparently so, but according to the landlady here nothing was ever proven, and no arrests were ever made.'

'Exactly my point,' says Ralph again. 'It's a huge mystery. And it's interesting that the townsfolk were so prejudiced against the fair workers that they still pointed fingers despite an investigation. They petitioned to prevent the good-for-local-business fair returning, again despite no proof of criminality. There must be residents who know more than they're letting on.'

'What's your theory?' I ask, although I suspect I know where he's going with it.

'Reading between the lines, I think the townsfolk know exactly who's to blame for the attacks – whether in '97 or '98 or both – but they've let the fair workers take the fall all this time. Talk about small-town bias against so-called outsiders. But the fair workers have a right to reply, and that's what I want in the book,' he says excitedly.

Now it's my turn to sigh. I was right; it sounds like a simple research trip merely gathering information is about to morph into a complex historic exploration. I'm not happy about the prospect even though I've currently got nowhere better to be. Still, Ralph doesn't know that and I've no intention of revealing I'm nursing a cracked heart and that I'm imminently homeless after splitting with Claudia. Although we've worked together for a few years now and got to know each other quite well, I have no desire to cross the boundary from colleague to friend.

Not with Ralph, and not with anybody. Like most writers, I prefer being a solitary creature, especially when it comes to my career.

'Except here's where I remind you that I'm a ghostwriter and not a journalist or a private investigator,' I say, my tone clipped.

'No, but Mason McKenzie *was* a journalist. He was all over the Sanderson story back in the day so how lucky are you that you're meeting with him this morning?'

'Oh-so lucky,' I say, deadpan.

'How about you put that smart mouth to good use by speaking to McKenzie and a few more of the locals?' he suggests but I can hear the amusement in his voice. Ralph is the nearest thing I've ever had to a father or big brother in a sense, and I suspect he enjoys our verbal sparring. Sometimes I do too. 'And while you're doing that,' he continues, 'I've also tasked Ebony with digging out anything that's been documented about the fair workers specifically, so she'll send you what she gets as she gets it. This is what this book needs, Allie – a bit of sensationalism! Everyone loves an unsolved cold case these days. And remember, once it's done, you'll get that series complete bonus I promised. Maybe treat yourself and Claudia to a well-deserved break somewhere better than sad old Stonethorpe-On-Sea.'

I nod against the phone, momentarily buoyed by the mention of the bonus while ignoring the sting of hearing Claudia's name. I'll need the money if I'm going to be paying rent on a new place by myself. I just need to get through the next few days, finish this project for Ralph and then move on to the next stage of my life, whatever that will look and feel like. After all, I'm nothing if not an expert in starting over.

'All right,' I say. 'I'll try to find some fresh dirt for you, as you put it, but you heard it from me: twenty-year-old cold cases rarely warm up again.'

'Good girl. But you never know – you could end up being the key to unlocking it all,' he says, and I can picture his wide-mouthed smile, his double chin creasing, and the manic expression he wears when he's enthused about something.

'I doubt that,' I reply, but as often is the case on our calls, he's already gone.

19TH MAY 1995

SCARLET

It was Dad's funeral today. It was so sad. Mum told me, Rubie and Rosalie that we had to be strong but then she clung to Uncle Silas like a limpet through the whole service, like her legs were too weak to stand on. How is she meant to look after us if she can't even hold herself up? A few people came back to the house afterwards for cups of tea that Rosalie and Mrs Roberts made for everyone, but they all just sat around whispering and acting sorry for us.

I went and sat on the wall outside to get away from them but then Uncle Silas and creepy Mr Roberts came outside too. I didn't mean to listen, but Uncle Silas's voice isn't exactly quiet, and I could hear him talking about an insurance policy or something. He kept looking back at the house and pointing at the barn and fields and Mr Roberts was smiling and nodding. But before I could creep closer to hear more Rubie found me and dragged me back inside and up to our bedroom. She locked the door behind us then started giggling and brought out a handful of money from inside her pillowcase. She said she had found a wallet in one of the coats downstairs and had taken it because anything in our home means it's "finders keepers" for us.

I was brave enough to tell her she should put it back, but she rolled her eyes and said that we needed all the money we could get because now Dad's dead, Mum's probably going to have to sell the house, and if that happens then all three of us will end up having to share a bedroom because there's no way Mum can afford to stay here. She said she didn't mind sharing a room with me but she'd rather die than share with Rosalie too. I didn't want to tell her what I heard Uncle Silas saying because I don't know what it means, so I just started crying. She called me a "fucking crybaby" and told me to get a grip. I hate her! She makes everything even worse than it already is. I'm really scared. What's going to happen to all of us now?

SATURDAY 28TH OCTOBER 2017

CHAPTER NINE

ALLIE

'It's nice to see a young woman enjoying her food,' comments Marla as I tuck into the scrambled eggs on toast that she served me soon after I arrived downstairs for breakfast. The dining room contains three small sets of tables and chairs but I'm the only one here. 'I don't care what I read or hear about carbs, you'd never stop me eating potatoes or bread.' She chuckles as she fusses at the sideboard moving the teapots, plates, cups, cutlery, jugs of milk and orange juice, and those small, individual boxes of cereal fractionally so they're just so. She seems a busy, pottering type of woman and judging by the cleanliness of the B&B, she does a decent job of looking after it, especially if it's just her with a bit of help from her son. There's a large, framed print on the wall above the sideboard, a vista of Stonethorpe-On-Sea's promenade from back in the day, dated 1975. The vibrant-looking scene is a far cry from the depressing derelict remains I saw last night.

'Nor me,' I lie in response to her statement. No need to mention that I often restrict my intake when the scales show that I'm carrying an extra pound or two above my preferred weight. Luckily, genetics plays a welcome part in enabling me to maintain my figure; Mum was always petite and slim.

'More coffee, dear?' asks Marla. I shake my head and check the time on my phone.

'No thanks, I need to get going,' I say, draining my cup.

'Can I give you directions anywhere? We don't have any tourist attractions as such these days but there are some nice walking spots with lovely views.'

I stand and unhook my jacket and bag from the back of the chair before sliding my phone into the back pocket of my jeans.

'No thanks,' I say again. 'I'm not a tourist, remember.' Recalling my conversation with Ralph and his insistence that I speak to more of the locals, and Marla's helpful gossiping yesterday, I offer her another snippet of information. 'I've actually got a meeting with Mason McKenzie this morning so I'm heading straight there.'

Marla puts down the coffee pot and raises her eyebrows. 'Mason McKenzie the journalist?'

I nod. 'Well, former journalist.'

The landlady tenses, eyeing me warily. 'Are you really a journalist too?' she asks. Her reaction implies a dislike of Mason, which only makes me more interested in what he's got to say. If I'm being forced to meet with him, better that the conversation's not a boring one.

'No, I'm not. As I said, I'm currently writing books about seaside towns. The one I'm working on now focuses on the decline of tourism.' I smile. It's not technically a lie.

She softens slightly. 'Well, you've come to the right place here, dear, and I'm sure Mr McKenzie will happily enlighten you on the reasons why the tourists dropped off like lemmings off a cliff. I mean, he's made a career out of it ever since the Sanderson incident. Talk about milking it – case in point that newspaper article about the anniversary.' She purses her lips and gestures to the reception desk in the hallway where the stack of papers still sits. 'I do still worry about those girls never being able to move on, what with it being dragged up and gossiped about year on year.' She tuts, seemingly oblivious to the fact that she's doing her fair share of the dragging. 'They still live in the same house, you know? How are they ever supposed to escape the past if they're constantly surrounded by it and reminded of it? Personally, I think they'd have been better off leaving Stonethorpe altogether but the way they are now... it's just not that easy for them by all accounts. There's some that believe the attack may have been sexually motivated too.' She shakes her head. 'Those poor girls. Rapists deserve castration if you ask me.'

Although I don't comment on her bold opinion, I silently agree with her. However, innocent babies are sometimes born as a consequence of rape, and I believe they deserve love and the chance of a good life.

'Right then, Mum,' calls a disembodied voice from the hallway. 'I'm off to the café.' A young man pops his head around the door frame. I'm surprised to see he's the ginger-haired kid from the pub. 'See you later,' he says to Marla then he notices me and grins.

'Oh, this is my son, Rye,' she says proudly as he steps into the room.

I wonder if it was him causing the creaks I heard on the landing last night.

'Hello again.' He shoves his hands in his pockets and nods towards me, as though doing a little bow.

'Again?' asks Marla, turning back to me with a mild look of horror, as though I'd purposely sought her son out on arrival. I know I might not look conventional, but mother hens don't need to worry about me corrupting their boys; only men on the more mature side interest me.

'We met briefly in The Smugglers,' explains Rye. 'Glad you got back okay,' he says to me, referencing my hasty exit last night. 'Silas can be a pain in the arse when he's on one. You shouldn't take any notice of him.'

'Oh, was he ranting again?' asks Marla with another tut and shake of her head as she begins clearing away my plate and cup, panic seemingly allayed. 'I'm sorry about that, dear. And Rye's right, take no notice whatsoever of that cantankerous old fool.'

I force a tight smile to offset the memory of the discomfort of Silas Sanderson's sinister stare. 'Well, I'd better get going,' I say, knowing it's a fifteen-minute drive to Mason's house across town.

'I'll walk you out,' offers the kid, moving to Marla and giving her a peck on the cheek. She beams at him. It's so sweet it's nauseating.

In the hallway, he bounds ahead to open the door for me, and I have to suppress the urge to laugh. He's like an eager puppy.

Outside, I ask, 'So, what's Rye short for – Ryan?'

'No, actually, it's Ryerson – my surname. But everyone's called me Rye since I was a teenager, and it just stuck.' He opens the gate for me too and we come to a standstill on the footpath.

'You're still a teenager now, aren't you?' I tease. I glance back at the B&B and spy Marla peering out of the front bay window. She raises a hand and waves, and I signal to Rye that she's there.

'Oi! I'll have you know I'm twenty this year,' he says, mock-offended while waving back at his mum.

I laugh at the perfect illustration of my point being proven. 'Currently still a teenager though, mummy's boy.'

A blotchy blush forms on his cheeks as embarrassment

radiates off him, but he rallies. 'What's your name then? I didn't catch it last night.'

'That's because I didn't give it.' I pause despite his obvious desperation to know it. 'It's Allie,' I say, finally relenting.

'Allie,' he repeats. 'What's that short for – Allison?'

'No, it's just Allie,' I say. He nods and looks out towards the sea, and I regard his side profile. There's no denying he's a good-looking kid but an unsettling feeling flutters inside me, like the way the air changes before a storm. 'You remind me of someone I used to know.' I articulate the thought without meaning to and it makes me shiver. I shove my hands into my coat pockets and frown. I haven't thought about *him* in a long time, yet the memory is always there, sitting in the distant shadows, watching me from afar.

'Someone you used to like?' he asks, turning back to face me, his expression pathetically hopeful.

'No, not really,' I say, wildly understating it.

His face instantly drops. 'But you like me, yeah?' His grin is resilient, and I laugh again despite myself. I wish I'd have been so casually confident at his age instead of the complete opposite.

'I don't even know you and I'm old enough to be your mum – just.'

'Well, maybe you should give me a chance... I could be your missing puzzle piece.'

It's a ridiculous phrase and a notion that I hate – the implication that someone isn't whole without another person to complete them – but the sincerity and softness with which he says it causes an unexpected surge of emotion. I blink rapidly to try to prevent tears forming, perplexed by how quickly the kid's got under my usually thick skin.

'I doubt that,' I say snippily, sniffing, shutting him down.

He shrugs it off with a smaller smile this time, but I clocked the brief wince beforehand; the rejection stung. I wonder if he's this overfamiliar with everyone or just strange women – or men – visiting his mum's B&B in this shitty seaside town. Maybe he's just bored and looking for a way to entertain himself. Maybe he's lonely. The thought makes me feel sad and I regret my harsh tone. He's just a kid, clearly brought up to be a bit more sensitive and trusting than I was at his age. Marla's done a good job with him either as well as or in spite of his late father. I hope it's the former.

'Anyway, mind how you go,' he says as he walks away. It's such an old man phrase that I smile again as I cross the road to my car. I'm just about to get in when I spot a man sitting on one of the nearby wooden benches that are dotted along the prom. He's wearing a beanie hat and just staring out to sea, looking like he's got the weight of the world on his shoulders. Or else he's depressed to simply be here. I can relate.

I start the car and head towards Mason McKenzie's house. The sooner this meeting is over the better – one completed task closer to going back to Leeds. Because as Dorothy famously said: there's no place like home.

CHAPTER TEN

RUBIE

Rubie drops her customers' orders into her old, worn tote bag and hooks it over her shoulder, making sure her hair isn't caught up in the straps. She smooths the long black strands down over her chest, making sure the front hangs over half of her face to conceal her scar. She has trimmed her own hair for nearly two decades, as well as Scarlet's, and is surprised neither of them have started to go grey yet. Rubie remembers what thick, glossy manes they both used to have, how much they used to enjoy braiding and curling each other's hair, primping and preening each other as though looking at their own reflections. They were shocked when Rosalie cut all her hair off, presumably determined to be "different". Now their hair is lank and thin but still jet black. At least something of the past versions of themselves remain.

There are only seven parcels to post this week and five of them are for items bought for less than £10. It's hardly worth the trek to the post office but Rubie relishes this time, her Saturday morning freedom slot. She always goes early in the day to avoid people. She still doesn't know which is worse: the sneaky glances or the outright stares like she's some sort of circus curiosity. Still, the trip reminds her that she is actually part of the human race, even if it doesn't often feel that way anymore.

'I'll be back soon,' she says to Dot. Of course she will; where else could she – would she – go?

Their housekeeper nods, her still nimble hands deftly kneading the bread she bakes every week as she gazes out of the window towards the chicken coop in the back garden. A shabby picket fence pointlessly borders the lawn from the fields beside and behind it. There's no need for the border as all the land belongs to the farmhouse, as well as the barn and the small outbuildings to the right. Dot described the view as "pleasant enough" once but Rubie's sick of the sight of it day in, day out, year in, year out.

So far, Dot's the only one to make it past six months in the job and Rubie hopes she'll stick it out. She's generally a stern woman of few words, which isn't a bad thing, and it'd be good for Scarlet to finally have some long-term consistency. Plus, Dot doesn't seem to be intimidated by Silas in the slightest, which makes a change. They've had a high turnover of housekeepers due to their gnarly, prone to ranting, fierce uncle. One timid woman didn't even last a full day before slipping out without a word to any of them. And they've fallen foul of others who only came to glean inside gossip for the townsfolk, fuelling the rumours and prejudice. Dot, thankfully, seems sincere, solid and dependable.

Rubie takes the long way round to the post office, avoiding the fateful shortcut across the field as always. She's never walked that way again since it happened. The taxi driver drove them past it on the way home from the hospital and there were bunches of flowers and printed pictures and laminated signs tied to the fence with string or tie wraps. She often wondered what the messages said but by the time she was well enough to leave the house again, that spot was the last place she wanted to go. She preferred to fantasise about the note, or perhaps love poem, she was sure Felton had left her, the only genuine one amongst the no doubt clichéd and insincere missives from the townspeople.

Now, Rubie thinks about Felton again. About how differently her life could have turned out if fate hadn't stepped in and ruined her face and her future. She should have a husband by now, a family of her own. Sleepless nights, sticky little palms reaching out for her, tooth fairy visits, Sunday lunches around the kitchen table, teenage tantrums, GCSE revision sessions, Christmas mornings eagerly ripping shiny paper off carefully wrapped gifts. She wanted it all and she'll never have any of it. She aches with the bitter loss of it.

Pushing open the door of the post office, in the street off the main town square, Rubie enters the small familiar shop. Passing the front section, which houses balls of wool and spools of ribbon and packs of needles, she walks past the shelves of stationery and greeting cards, which haven't been restocked in years, and stops at the counter.

'Hello, Rubie, love,' says Maeve, the postmistress, her usual booming tone invading the quiet space. 'And how are you today? How's everything at the farm?' Her beady gaze rakes over Rubie, probably eager for a behind-the-scenes snippet of the Sandersons' lives.

But Rubie simply shrugs, as she always does. She keeps her exposed eye down as she stacks her parcels on the counter, choosing to stonewall Maeve, knowing that she loves to run her mouth to all and sundry. And even if Maeve wasn't a gossip, Rubie feels that she herself is too inept at conversation with anyone other than Scarlet anyway.

'First class as usual?' Maeve asks as she opens the hatch to take the parcels.

Rubie nods.

'Right you are, love.'

Maeve works efficiently, weighing and stickering and jabbing at the till's screen. 'Have you heard about our new visitor?' she asks with a playful twitch of her lips.

Rubie posts ten-pound notes through the gap in the bottom of the Plexiglass and shakes her head.

'Well,' says the older woman, stringing out the word and peering at Rubie over the top of her glasses, 'she's a writer. Poking around in the town's history apparently.'

A sudden spike of anxiety stabs Rubie in the chest and clearly travels straight to her face judging by Maeve's sympathetic look.

'Don't you worry, love, I'm sure she's not here to rake over what happened to you and that poor sister of yours. And if she does, well, she'll get short shrift from us locals!'

Rubie forces a polite smile as she collects her change and turns to leave, the conversation serving as a reminder of the scrutiny that still constantly follows her and Scarlet. *We're never going to escape it, are we?* she thinks.

As she leaves the post office, empty-handed now after folding and pocketing her tote bag, a gust of wind blows back her curtain of hair, exposing her right eye and cheek. Her inner programming makes her want to immediately smooth it back down, to cover her face, but she stops herself. For a moment she just stands there with her eyes closed, facing the sea, feeling the most "normal" she's felt in years, with the salty breeze stroking her skin and whipping long strands of hair behind her. The sensation takes her breath away and she could cry at the incongruity between fantasy and reality.

In her peripheral vision, Rubie notices a car approaching the mini roundabout to her right and instantly turns inwards to conceal her face and readjust her hair. Her moment of bliss is over. Shoving one hand in the empty pocket of her thin coat and holding the ends of her hair in her other fist to keep it secure, she sets off down the path before abruptly stopping again just seconds later, a familiar sight arresting her.

She watches as Silas approaches The Smugglers, his gait already wonky, his hacking cough clearly audible above the car's engine, the restless waves and swooping gulls. It's barely 11am. A cold shiver runs down Rubie's spine. The earlier he starts drinking, the more unpredictable he becomes, and she can never be sure what mood or state he'll be in when he returns home. Always wanting to be where her uncle is not, Rubie waits until he disappears through the pub's double doors then picks up her pace, eager to get back to Scarlet and the temporary solace of the farmhouse.

Dot nods her greeting as Rubie walks back into the kitchen.

'How's Scarlet?' she asks first, as always.

Drying her hands on a tea towel, the housekeeper jerks her head towards the window. Beyond, Scarlet is just visible in the chicken run in the back corner of the garden, sitting cross-legged with the silkies in front of their coop.

Dot collects her coat from one of the hooks near the back stable door. 'I'll be off. See you Monday,' she says, keeping her words to a minimum as usual.

Rubie nods, returning her gaze to the scene outside. 'Thank you, Dot.'

A minute later, the sisters are home alone again. The silence of the farmhouse feels heavy, but it is a familiar weight, as are the complex feelings Rubie has carried all these years. Her tangled thoughts wander back to Maeve's comments about the writer. The possibility that a stranger is digging into Stonethorpe's history – and by definition their own history – stirs up even more anxieties. It's bad enough being faced –

literally – with a perpetual reminder of the past and she doesn't want it dredged up and presented to the wider public again now. News of the writer has only intensified Rubie's sense of being watched and judged. Even if she's not here for her and Scarlet specifically, there are plenty of secrets to unearth, even more events that could come to light, if the rabid gossipmongers are to be believed. And they are secrets that could break the fragile forcefield Rubie's built around herself in one sharp, shattering blow.

CHAPTER ELEVEN

ALLIE

Mason McKenzie's sleek, white-rendered and grey-cladded dormer bungalow sits beyond fancy electric gates and contrasts starkly against the dreary Stonethorpe sky. As I pull up next to the intercom, I cast my eye over its neat modern façade, a huge picture window taking pride of place below an apex roof, a handsome porch housing double front doors to its left. *If this is the kind of place a former journalist and now lecturer can afford, it might be time to consider changing careers,* I muse to myself. Then I remember this is Stonethorpe-On-Sea and its negative history has ensured house prices have plummeted. The equivalent in Leeds would be a two-bed terrace near the city centre, which still costs a lot more than I can currently afford. All the more reason to get this series completion bonus from Ralph.

After opening my car window, I reach out and press the intercom button. 'Allie Sawyer,' I announce.

The speaker crackles before an inviting voice replies, 'Welcome, Allie. I'll meet you at the front door.'

I hear a click, and the gates slowly slide open, leaving me free to drive along the curved, brick-paved driveway to the house's entrance. One of the doors opens and out steps a tall, athletic, good-looking man. He must be in his mid-forties but clearly keeps himself in shape. He raises a hand in greeting before stepping back and holding the door wide open as I exit my car and walk towards him. I step inside the house, into a space filled with warm wooden tones contrasted with contemporary wall art, the scent of freshly brewed coffee welcoming me. Mason shakes my hand but doesn't try to kiss me hello, which I appreciate. As an ex-journalist he must know how to read people and has probably correctly gauged that I'm not one for affectionate greetings with strangers. I like him already.

'Good to meet you. Come on through,' he says, heading towards the arched opening at the end of the wide hallway. He's undeniably attractive – perhaps it's his genuine smile or his confident demeanour, or maybe it's his toned body and great arse. Annoyingly, my latter observations are immediately chased away by thoughts of Claudia. I consciously divert them before I descend into a pointless spiral about whose arse she might be checking out now. It's no longer any of my business.

Mason's kitchen is streamlined but sophisticated with a floor-to-ceiling window overlooking a large, manicured garden. It looks like it could be a centre spread in a glossy interior design magazine, but its clean lines and sharp edges with very few soft touches screams single man. It's a stark contrast to the more understated, suburban vibe of the rest of the street, like he's trying to make it obvious that he doesn't quite fit in or even belong here in Stonethorpe-On-Sea. If that's his intention, I like that about him – a man who's confident in his own style and not afraid to stand out.

He gestures for me to take a seat at the rustic wooden dining table in front of the window.

'Something to drink?' he asks. 'Tea, coffee? Something stronger?' He grins like we're sharing an inside joke, and I'm surprised to feel a faint flutter of interest. It's been a while since I've felt attracted to a man.

'Coffee. Thanks,' I reply as I set my phone down and open the recording app. He sits down too and pours us both coffee from the carafe already on the table, adding milk from the jug when I nod. His movements are relaxed, unhurried, adding to his air of confidence.

'Do you mind?' I ask, my finger hovering over my phone.

He slides my coffee towards me then leans back in his chair and smiles. 'Not at all. I'm an open book. Speaking of books, tell me about the one you're writing.'

Now it's my turn to smile at his unexpected segue as I press record. 'Ever the journalist, hmm? Well, I'm here to ask you questions, Mr McKenzie, not the other way round.'

He raises an eyebrow, amused. 'Fair enough. Go ahead. And call me Mason, please,' he says.

'Okay. Mason, I'll be straight with you. I'm ghostwriting a series of books about the darker side of travelling fairs. However, for this final instalment featuring Stonethorpe's Halloween fair, my client has decided he wants to feature the Sanderson case for some sensationalism.' I make exaggerated air quotes around the word "sensationalism" and roll my eyes, not bothering to conceal my feelings about the extra content. For some reason, I want him to know I'm my own person too.

Mason tilts his head, his interest clearly piqued. 'You don't think the case is relevant?'

I shrug. 'It's just... not what tickles my fancy. I'd rather write fiction. Novels. Create my own stories, not regurgitate a tired twenty-year-old cold case.'

'That tired twenty-year-old cold case kickstarted my entire career,' he says, a note of pride in his voice. 'But okay, I hear you. We all want to do something that tickles our fancy, as you say. Are you good at telling lies, Allie?'

I'm taken aback by the directness of his question, caught off guard momentarily. I take a sip of my coffee while I play for time, the rich taste a pleasing contrast to Marla's cheap instant at the B&B. 'Lies?' I ask.

'Yeah.' Mason leans forward, appraises me. 'Fibs, half-truths, words not rooted in evidence. Can you spin a good tale when it's not entirely factual? All writers need to be able to.'

'Can you?' I volley back. He laughs, the sound deep and pleasing.

'Sure,' he says. 'When I need to.'

'Everyone can when they need to,' I state. I consider something for a moment, unsure if I'm going to say it, but this isn't exactly a conventional interview, and I feel like we're having fun already. I decide to just blurt it out. 'In fact, I've got three statements for you. Two of them are true and one is a lie. Want to guess which is which?'

'Sure,' he repeats after a beat, tapping his index finger on the table. His eyes light up with curiosity, then with something else as I pause the recording.

'Okay,' I say, settling back into my chair, secretly delighted I've diverted his attention so easily. 'One: I had a long-term sugar daddy when I was in my twenties. Two: I'm bisexual. Three: I have a deep, dark secret in my past.'

Mason listens intently, his gaze fixed on me as he processes each of my shocking statements. He's clearly not easily ruffled; a trait I relate to. 'Hmm,' he muses thoughtfully, and I want to lift open the top of his head to see his inner workings. I'm enjoying his apparent fascination in me, the undeniable charge between us, this unexpected turn to the dull day I anticipated. 'The sugar daddy is the lie?' he says eventually.

I shake my head. 'Nope. The dark secret is the lie. Like the non-fiction I currently write, I'm an open book too.'

He nods, studying me intently. 'Interesting. Most people would probably find your forthrightness intimidating, Allie...'

'How do you find it?' I ask abruptly.

'Refreshing,' he states, holding my gaze as he takes a sip of his coffee.

I smile at the compliment. 'I guess it's a quality people either love or hate.'

'It's certainly intriguing,' says Mason, setting down his cup. 'Personally, I think it can only serve to make you a better writer. Gives you the ability to see things exactly how they are, without distortion or unnecessary embellishment. Much like a journalist.' He grins again.

The comment feels insightful, and it pleases me that he thinks we share common ground in that way after only just meeting. He's wrong but I do like that he sees me this way. I wonder if he's always been like this, able to foster such a comfortable atmosphere with whoever he speaks to, or whether I'm bringing out a different side of him. In his old line of work, it was probably the former, but I'm enjoying the way he's making me feel.

'So, what are you going to do once this book is written?' he asks, segueing back to the original conversation. I'm slightly disappointed to return to it after our brief flirty detour.

'Well, despite my client's prediction that this final instalment is going to rocket up the bestseller charts thanks to the Sanderson sisters' connection, I definitely don't want to write non-fiction anymore. My finishing bonus will go towards funding writing a novel full time, even if only for a few months.'

'Sounds like a plan,' he says. 'The best way out is often through.'

'A motto I live by.' I smile, feeling a strong sense of camaraderie with this man. I shift in my seat and take another gulp of coffee, pressing record on my phone again. 'So, what brought you to Stonethorpe in the first place – your journalism work?'

'I actually lived here when I was a boy,' he reveals. 'We moved to London when my dad got a new job, and we stayed. I went to uni there – King's College. The Sanderson case brought me back here often, just after I started working on my first paper. I asked to cover it.'

'So you were the reason the story spread far and wide?'

He nods, a proud expression on his face. 'I guess I was. It intrigued me anyway, but the fact it happened in my old home town even more so.'

'Yet despite the nationwide coverage, this high-profile case remains unsolved,' I state, surprising myself by sounding like a proper interviewer. 'Why is that, do you think?'

Before he can answer, a phone rings. He crosses over to the kitchen island and picks up his mobile. 'Will you excuse me please, Allie? I need to take this.'

I press pause on my own phone again and he heads out of the kitchen. I hear him saying 'Hello, darling' as he enters the hall, and I feel a surprising sense of disappointment. He doesn't seem the type who'd be willing to cheat so I guess I must have imagined our chemistry. The plunging realisation turns my mood instantly sour.

'Sorry,' he says, returning to the room a few minutes later. 'I never refuse my daughter's calls. She still lives with her mum in London, so I don't get to see her as much as I'd like. She'll be with me for Christmas this year though...' He looks at me shyly. 'Sorry,' he repeats. 'I always get a bit gooey when I talk about her.'

'You share custody?' I ask.

He nods. 'It's not always easy but it's worth it. My ex-wife and I are on good terms now, but she hated living here. She's something of a social butterfly and needs the hustle and bustle of a big city to sustain her. I might move back to London myself one day, if the right job ever comes up, but for now my daughter gets to experience the best of both worlds. What about you, Allie... do you have a family?'

I feel a pang of loneliness as I think about Claudia. She's the closest I've come to having a family in my whole adult life even though we lasted barely a year. Then I think about Story's furry face and smile. 'Not in the conventional sense,' I answer cryptically, not wanting to go into detail. Enigmatic is my default setting, however attracted I am to someone initially.

'Anyway,' I say, pressing record for the third time, recalling Ralph's order to dig up fresh dirt, 'let's get back to the topic I'm here to discuss. What are your theories about the Sanderson case?'

He tops up our half-empty cups and settles back in his chair. 'How long have I got you for because I have lots of thoughts?'

Claudia's face flashes before my eyes again and I blink it away. Then I think of my empty room at the B&B, the deserted promenade, the pub full of locals including ranty Silas Sanderson, and I realise I'm glad to be here instead. I smile at Mason. 'You've got me for as long as you want me.'

'That's good to know,' he says, smiling too.

CHAPTER TWELVE

FENIX

The jingle of the bell above the post-office door stirs something inside Fenix, an echo of Christmases past. In his mind's eye he can see baby Milly banging tunelessly on a xylophone, her chubby hands springing up and down, while he and Janelle over-celebrate her basic musical efforts as though she was a child prodigy. He wonders if this Christmas will be his last and his heart aches painfully at the thought of missing many more of his daughter's milestones in the years to come.

The inside of the shop smells musty, a typical scent that clings to places like this, a unique and recognisable combination of paper and ink, wool and wood. And it's so cool and quiet, like a tomb. The whole town is much quieter than he remembers without the bucket-and-spade tourists descending on the caravan park in the summer, and the annual Halloween fair bringing its colour and crowds and chaos. The thick silence unsettles him, makes him feel strangely exposed, even in this old, small, cluttered post office. But he's here for a reason and he needs to see that reason through.

His boots scuff against the worn lino as he approaches the

counter. The postmistress doesn't even glance up from the magazine she's reading. He's the only customer and it's only when he steps directly in front of her and clears his throat softly, does she finally acknowledge him.

'Oh, hello there, love. What can I do for you?' She leans forward, resting her ample bosom on her crossed forearms and giving him a once-over that's impressively both inquisitive and indifferent. Her curly grey hair forms a cloud on her head and her bright fuchsia lipstick has bled into the deep lines around her mouth.

He hesitates, the question lodged in his throat, almost choking him, even though he's mentally rehearsed asking it over and over. He's here for answers, after all.

He coughs into his fist, draws on his inner courage. 'Bit of a weird request but I was wondering,' he begins, his voice careful, 'if you knew how I could get in touch with Rosalie Sanderson.'

The woman's pencilled-in brows knit together behind her large glasses, curiosity written all over her face. She purses her lips as she considers her response. The Sanderson sisters are practically an urban legend in this town, but he doubts there are many who mention Rosalie's name alongside Rubie's and Scarlet's. The woman's reaction confirms this.

'Rosalie?' she repeats, turning the corners of her mouth down. 'Well, she ran off, didn't she. Not long after you know what.' She bobs her head several times, assuming Fenix knows exactly what she's talking about. He nods back. 'Yes, she just upped and left, with a secret beau by all accounts. Never came back. Put that poor ailing mother of hers through even more heartache.' The woman gives a sniff of disapproval.

'A boyfriend?' asks Fenix, frowning. 'I don't suppose you know of anyone who might know where she is now? Or him, even?'

The postmistress shrugs. 'Some say she's up north somewhere. Some claim she's abroad. Nobody actually knows anything for sure, about her or who she went off with. He can't have been a local or we'd have known who else was missing, wouldn't we? Put two and two together – or one and one!' She barks an amused sound at her own joke. 'But I can tell you that the one place she isn't living is in that old farmhouse with her sisters and uncle.'

Fenix processes the information. Ran off? He assumed she'd have left town but he can't find any trace of her online. When he'd first plucked up the courage to google her, he'd expected to find links to career successes or at least a social media profile but she doesn't seem to exist in cyber space. It's as though she's been erased. The running away story sounds simple enough – too simple perhaps – but he knows that most people don't just disappear without a reason. Especially not teenage girls with severely injured sisters and an ill mother.

'The farmhouse?' he asks, trying to keep his voice as neutral as he can.

The woman's gaze is sharp now, assessing him with a different kind of interest. 'Yes. Why? Are you thinking of paying a visit?'

Fenix shrugs like it's neither here nor there. 'Maybe. Might someone there have a contact address for her?'

The postmistress regards him for a moment longer. Then she sighs and scribbles something down on the back of an envelope. 'There,' she says, sliding it under the partition. 'But don't expect too much. Rubie and Silas aren't exactly personable and Scarlet, well, nobody's heard a peep out of her for two decades.'

'Thanks,' says Fenix, pocketing the already familiar address. He'd hoped not to have to return to it but realises now it was inevitable all along. He spots a card on the narrow rack next to the counter and instinctively grabs it. The bouquet of red roses on the front feels apt.

After paying for the card, he turns to leave and hears the bell jingle again. Marla, the landlady from the B&B walks in, bundled up in a woollen coat and knitted scarf. Her cheeks are rosy from the cold and her expression is as cheerful as her voice.

'Fenix!' she exclaims, clearly delighted to see him again. 'Fancy bumping into you here.'

He smiles politely. 'Hello, Marla.'

Marla turns her attention to the other woman. 'Maeve, you've got to meet this lovely young man. He's one of my guests at the B&B.'

'Fenix? What an odd name,' says Maeve rudely.

'If you think that's strange, I've got a writer staying with me too and she's got pink hair! Can you believe it?' Marla laughs. 'My Bruce would have had a twinkle in his eye at the sight of her. Writers though – you know what they say... be careful what you say around them, or they'll put you in their book! Mind you, she is writing one about this town so we'd better be in it!'

Maeve and Marla cackle like witches while Fenix wonders about the mysterious writer. A woman with pink hair in a small town like this? Surely she'll be hard to miss. He'll no doubt cross paths with her soon enough. Maybe she's here for a reason related to the Sanderson sisters too. Maybe she'll be able to help him locate Rosalie?

'Catch you later, ladies,' he says, exiting the shop as quickly and as smoothly as he can.

Outside, the cold sea air nips his face, but he pulls out his phone and stares at his screensaver for a moment. It's a blurry photo Milly took of herself when he took his eyes off her for just a minute. She's such a mischievous, beautiful girl, he can barely believe he's responsible for half of her DNA. He makes a call and Janelle answers after a few rings, her familiar lilt so warm but so distant.

'Hey, you. Everything okay?' she asks.

'Everything's fine,' he confirms. 'I just wanted to hear your voice.'

There's a pause, a slight tension. She's the only one who knows why he's here, why he felt he had to return to this now sleepy seaside town that possesses the defining story of his past. How much he needs to lay his ever-present ghosts to rest now that he's managed to wrestle his demons into submission.

'You can just come home, you know,' she says softly after a few seconds, interpreting his tone so perfectly like she always does, always has. She's a better woman than he deserves, and he still marvels that they found each other six years ago. Two lost souls uniting. 'You've paid your penance. You're a good man now.'

Fenix places one hand on his head, his fingers splayed on top of his beanie hat, as if to help keep her kind words contained in his brain. She's always believed in the power of redemption. That people can change. That second chances can be earned. Yet he's never quite managed to convince himself of that.

'I know,' he replies, like he does whenever she says that, so grateful for her. 'But I've got a lead now and you know how much I want to make amends.'

'Just don't get lost following your lead, okay? You're already far enough away from us, and Milly misses you. I do too.'

'I miss you both so much. I'll be home soon.'

She sighs gently on the other end of the line. 'We love you, Fenix.'

'I love you too, my gorgeous girls. More than anything,' he says, meaning every word. They say goodbye and conscious that Marla could emerge from the post office at any moment and delay him further, he ends the call.

For a few moments he stares out at the choppy sea and the hazy grey horizon, thinking about the blank greeting card stowed in his bag. Taking a deep, fortifying breath, he sets off in the direction of the Sanderson house. It's time to face whoever or whatever comes next.

31ST OCTOBER 1995

SCARLET

This has been the worst birthday ever! Everything is so messed up! Mum sat us down last night to tell us that she has been diagnosed with something called multiple sclerosis, or MS for short. I don't know what it is but of course Rosalie did. She grabbed Mum's hands, making me and Rubie look really stupid and uncaring! Mum said she'll probably have more bad days than good but it's not something that will ever go away. She told us last night so as not to ruin our birthday but how were we supposed to be happy today? She's already so weak and tired all the time and asked us to help more around the house. Saint Rosalie said she'll create a rota, which I could tell annoyed Rubie, but she didn't say anything in front of Mum. Good luck to Rosalie trying to make Rubie do anything she doesn't want to do, even if it's for Mum!

And if that wasn't bad enough, Maple's gone too. Uncle Silas arrived last night and when I woke up this morning the barn was empty except for the stacks of hay and the rabbit hutches. I cried because I felt so bad about being cross with her for a long time, but she was a good horse and what happened to Dad was just a horrible accident. Uncle Silas said he "took care of her", but I *don't know what that means exactly. I wish I could have said goodbye.*

We couldn't even go to the Halloween fair tonight because Uncle Silas said no. He's not our dad but he's visiting more and always telling us what we can and can't do! Rubie's brave enough to answer back to him, which he hates, but today he raised his hand to her as though he was going to hit her! His face was as red as a tomato! She dared him to do it but then Mum shouted for help from the kitchen, so he didn't.

The ONLY good thing that happened today was that Rosalie helped Mum bake our birthday cake. It was chocolate – my favourite! I only had a small piece though. Rubie says I need to watch my weight because I'm getting a "muffin top". Another of her sayings that I don't understand. I bet she just makes them up most of the time to confuse me and make me feel bad.

I really, really, really miss Dad. I went out to the oak tree in the field behind the barn to talk to him for a while. I like to think that his ashes have mingled into the roots and the trunk and he's now part of the tree and watching over us, just as big and strong as he was when he was alive. Today would have been fun if he was still here. He would have taken us to the fair and won us a cuddly toy each just like last year!

SATURDAY 28TH OCTOBER 2017

CHAPTER THIRTEEN

ALLIE

As Mason begins talking about the Sanderson case and his investigation into it, I watch him with a slight smirk. He projects such an easy confidence with a hint of brooding intensity. He still talks about it so passionately even after all these years. His famous watershed story.

'So, what in particular got you so obsessed?' I ask.

He shrugs, but not because he doesn't know. 'Well, it's a hell of a conundrum, isn't it? A small seaside town where everyone knows everyone, an annual fair that passes without event for decades then two teenage sisters are suddenly struck down and left for dead during fair week. No apparent motive. No witnesses. I mean, that's a mystery in itself, right?'

I nod.

'Especially as nothing really changed on the face of it. Yet everything did. The rumours, the suspicions, the outright finger-pointing at the fair workers who hotfooted it out of here. They were the prime suspects. A dome of fear seemed to descend upon the town and the Clifton boys got lumped into the suspect pool because they were close mates with so many of the fair workers. Sandy Crest – their parents' caravan park – struggled massively in the aftermath, causing even more consternation among the locals, especially the other business owners who also relied on the out-of-towners that the fair brought in.'

'But rightly so that they were all lumped together if these Cliftons did have anything to do with the attack on the sisters?' I state.

'Yet there was no evidence to suggest they did,' he says. 'No hard evidence but also no alibis, except them vouching for each other. A double negative in the police's eyes, but still not enough to warrant an arrest. And then there was another one.'

'Another one what?' I ask, leaning forward, although I already know from what Marla told me. Still, I want his version for the recording, for the reference.

Mason hooks his gaze onto mine. 'After Rubie and Scarlet were attacked in '97 and nobody was brought to justice for the crime, the locals got spooked. They petitioned to ban the fair ever coming back despite the further detrimental effect it would have on the town's economy. But it didn't work. The council pushed back, and the fair rolled into town again in '98 like nothing had happened. And then in '98 another girl was attacked. This time in one of the caravans on the Sandy Crest site itself. That's when things really blew up. The town turned against the fair for good after that and their second bigger petition, including many impassioned speeches at council meetings, got the ban secured,' he says.

'What happened to the girl in the caravan?' I ask.

'She survived, like Rubie and Scarlet did. But it was bad and a diversion from the original attacks as the second one appeared to be sexually motivated.'

I let out a low whistle to lighten the atmosphere more than anything else. The air in the room feels heavier somehow. We sit in silence, our imaginations painting appalling pictures neither of us wants to see.

'That's pretty dark. And what about the Sanderson sisters?' I ask. 'You said they survived but what actually happened to them?'

Mason sighs, running a hand through his hair. 'Tragedy after tragedy. Their mother died not long after the attack. Brain haemorrhage, if I remember correctly, although she'd been battling MS for years. Her brother, Silas, came back to look after the girls but the guy's a piece of work – a religious nutter and a drunk. For the past twenty years Rubie has barely left the house and the only people who have set eyes on Scarlet are the numerous housekeepers that Silas regularly sees off.'

'Tragic indeed,' I say.

'There was another sister too. Rosalie.' Mason tugs at his lips, his gaze drifting out the window. 'She's who intrigued me the most. But she disappeared while Rubie and Scarlet were still in the hospital. Silas claimed she had a secret boyfriend and ran off with him, that she bolted selfishly while her mother was too busy worrying about her sisters. She wrote home a few months later, not knowing her mother had died, and Silas showed the letter to the police. But nothing ever came of it. I tried to track her down but had no luck either. She's a ghost.' He shrugs again. 'I'm a damn good journalist but I don't have access to the same manpower and resources that the police do. Plus, back then the power of the internet wasn't what it is now.'

'So nobody actually dug that deeply into the case?' I ask, raising an eyebrow. 'Sounds suspicious to me.'

'Me too. I wondered if a copper was in on it for a while but again, I only hit dead ends on that score. The town didn't want anyone to dig deeper. It just wanted to close ranks and close down.'

I reflect on that for a moment. It makes sense. Small towns bury ugly stuff from outsiders. The Sanderson sisters and the other poor girl are definitely ugly stuff. This is gold for Ralph's book, even if it's not what I signed up for. It still feels a bit icky to me but he's going to love these gritty embellishments. Still, something about it gives me the chills. Teenage girls don't seem to fare too well in Stonethorpe-On-Sea.

Mason seems to sense my mood shift because he stands up and walks to a drawer across the kitchen. He retrieves a folder and drops a handful of neatly cut out newspaper articles from inside it onto the table.

I look at his collection. All his bylines. His curated evidence of the grisly content Ralph thinks he needs to boost sales of the book series. Ebony is probably gathering copies of all these together too, but I like the idea of referring to Mason's originals. Perhaps I can borrow them, give myself a reason to come back.

As though reading my mind, he says, 'I can make copies of these for you?' He flashes me a smile, one that feels warm and personal. 'If you want to collect them, I can have them ready tomorrow evening?' he suggests.

I smile back, certain I've interpreted his invitation correctly. 'Sure,' I say coolly. 'That'd be helpful.'

Mason sits back down. 'You know, while you're here, there are a few other people you might want to talk to. For wider context.'

'Such as?' I ask. I'll cross-reference his recommendations with the list Ebony's already emailed.

'Well, for starters, old Maeve at the post office. She's got her finger on the pulse of this town. Massive gossip, though, so don't treat everything she says as gospel, but if you sift carefully through the silo of shit she spouts, there'll be a few gold nuggets. Caroline and Phillip Roberts too. They own the land the fair used to be built on and live in a house next to it. Their family has been here for generations, and they were tight with the Cliftons who owned Sandy Crest back in the day. All the Cliftons are long gone now though, including the boys Felton and Colton.'

I nod, mentally filing the names away even though I'm still recording our conversation. 'Anyone else?'

Mason's expression turns sly. 'Possibly the vicar, Reverend Kiely. He's only been here about ten years or so, but he might know how to contact the previous vicar who arrived in 1997, just before everything went to hell. Some say he knew more than he let on about what happened back then, but of course he always hid behind the cloak of confidentiality.'

I raise an eyebrow. 'The vicar? Seriously?'

He shrugs. 'This is a small town, Allie. Everyone has secrets.'

There's a brief silence before Mason clears his throat. His Adam's apple bobs and I imagine pressing my lips gently against it, feeling the warmth of his skin. I shake my head, reminding myself there's a time and a place. Maybe that time and place will be here tomorrow night.

'You could also try speaking to the local police. See if they'll let you look at the old case files or maybe talk you through the investigation. I'm not sure how helpful they'll be but—'

I cut him off. 'I told you – I'm not here to investigate the full cold case, Mason. I'm here to ghost-write a book about the downsides of travelling fairs. What happened here twenty years ago is terrible, but it'll fill one or two chapters, tops. This book as a whole still needs to fit in with the rest of the series.'

Mason holds his hands up, palms towards me, and I realise that came out a little sharper than I intended.

'Fair enough,' he says. 'Just thought I'd throw it out there.'

I nod. There's a difference between researching a book and

playing at being a bonafide detective, which I'm not and don't want to be. I'm just here to do a writing job and get paid for it.

'Thanks anyway but I'll be sticking to what I'm good at,' I say, leaning back in my chair and crossing my arms.

Mason's eyes gleam with something unreadable but he doesn't push it any further. Instead, he shifts the conversation back to slightly lighter topics like how the landscape of the town has changed since the fair stopped and the caravan park closed down. We fall back into a casual rhythm, the tension dissipating as we continue to chat, the underlying current of attraction flowing pleasantly between us.

A while later, as we wrap up, Mason gathers together the newspaper articles still fanned out on the table. He clutches them in one hand as I turn off the recording. We've been talking for nearly two hours. 'So, tomorrow evening then?'

I appreciate his bold move. 'Tomorrow evening,' I repeat. 'I'll swing by.' Then, not one for beating around the bush, I look him square in the face and tell him, 'But just so we're clear, it'll be a one-time only exchange.'

Mason's smile widens as he picks up on my meaning, his eyes dark and mischievous. 'If you say so.'

There's something about the way he says it that makes my stomach flip again. I'm glad we understand each other though. Just a bit of fun, no strings attached.

I stand, pocketing my phone. He walks me to the door, dropping the articles onto the kitchen counter on the way.

'7pm?' he asks, referring to tomorrow night.

I nod, a knowing smile playing on my lips, before stepping out into the crisp October air. It cools my flushed skin and defuses the heat that's been building between us as I walk to my car, climb in and start the engine. I can feel his eyes on me the whole time. And then an image of Rubie and Scarlet Sanderson walking home through a dark field hijacks my thoughts. Did they sense someone watching them the night they were attacked too? I shake the visual from my head, remind myself yet again I'm not getting pulled into a cold case, and drive through Mason's electric gates, already looking forward to my return visit.

CHAPTER FOURTEEN

ALLIE

The bell above the door jingles as I step inside the post office and scan the dim surroundings. It's a tired time capsule in here and sitting behind the counter, like a waxwork dummy, is presumably the postmistress, Maeve. Her reading glasses are perched on the end of her thin nose and as I approach, I see she has one of those women's trash mags spread open in front of her. One of the ones with the shocking stories such as *I Married My Hamster!* Or *My Mum Framed Me For Murder!* It's the kind of magazine the Sanderson story would have been suited to, I think unkindly.

She swings her gaze towards me, annoyance – presumably at being interrupted – morphing immediately into curiosity.

'Well, if it isn't our visiting writer,' she says in an over-familiar mocking tone.

I'm not surprised she knows who I am after Mason's not so complimentary description of her being the town's biggest gossip. And small towns have an uncanny way of spreading news faster than Facebook.

I force a smile despite her slight frostiness and decide to dispense with the pleasantries. 'Mason McKenzie sent me your way. He suggested you might be able to help me with a bit of background about Stonethorpe-On-Sea.'

'For a book?' she asks, fishing for more information.

'Yes,' I confirm, without elaboration.

She closes her magazine and leans forward conspiratorially, seemingly interested now. 'You know, I aways thought Mr McKenzie himself would have written a book. He could have made a killing out of all that Sanderson sisters business. I mean, he wrote enough articles about it, would have been easy enough to create a paperback.'

She makes a good point in theory. 'Why didn't he, do you think?' I ask, not only genuinely interested, but to make her think her opinion holds weight. I might not be an interviewer, but I can steer certain people well enough now.

'Well, he's a local too, so a book would have probably been a step too far. It's one thing reporting news but quite another trying to profit off a tragedy in the very town you live in. Distasteful,' she says pointedly.

I flush, feeling slightly awkward on Ralph's behalf. He might never have been to Stonethorpe, but he is trying to profit off this story for his *Forgotten Fairground* series. Maeve's right – it is distasteful.

'Mason believes the two are interlinked – the fair and the Sanderson case – but the book I've been commissioned to write is more about the annual Halloween fair and its negative effects on the town itself,' I say. A half-truth to both ingratiate and defend myself, neither of which I should have to do. Damn Ralph and his "fresh dirt".

Maeve's eyes gleam behind her glasses and I can sense her floodgates are about to burst open, all frostiness melted away. That didn't take much but, like I say, I'm good at guiding people in the direction I want them to go. 'It is all interlinked,' she states emphatically. 'The fair, the Cliftons, the Sandersons, the attacks, the aftermath.' She holds up a finger for each one. 'Outsiders like ghouls and vultures, picking over everything, which was more than the police themselves bothered to do. What a shambles. They ought to be ashamed of themselves. But we know what happened and we've protected ourselves ever since.' She jabs her index finger at her chest. 'No more fairs. No more fair workers. No more tourists en masse. I mean, it's closing the stable door after the horse has bolted, mind, but there haven't been any more major crimes on our watch.' She straightens post-monologue, looking proud.

'Was it really that bad – the fair?' I ask.

Maeve scoffs. 'Bad? It caused utter chaos every single year. Brought nothing but trouble starting with petty thefts and parking disputes, escalating to harassment and intimidation of local shop owners and youngsters, especially the girls, and then ending with those vicious attacks on the Sandersons and that other poor love.'

I nod, frowning. 'So how did the fair affect the caravan park's business? I mean, before the attack on the third girl the year after the Sandersons?'

Maeve takes a breath, clearly preparing herself for another diatribe. 'If you ask me, the Cliftons were tight with the fair workers, especially the two lads Felton and Colton who seemed to revel in being part of a bigger gang. The caravan park always made a killing during fair week, which pleased their father no end as he always hiked the prices right up. Fancied himself an astute businessman when it was just the basic principle of supply and demand for a repeat annual event. As long as he was making money, he didn't care who rented his caravans, or what happened inside them, by all accounts. Him and them boys of his... all bad apples.' She scowls, clucking her tongue.

'Did either Rubie or Scarlet Sanderson ever point fingers at anyone in particular?' I press.

Maeve throws up her hands. 'No! Neither ever once named and shamed but we all knew. And we made sure they knew we knew!'

The satisfaction in her voice makes my skin prickle. Mason's account of events was diluted compared to Maeve's venom-filled version, and she hasn't finished yet. 'It took a year, and another attack on another innocent victim, but we got rid of all of them. The fair, the fair workers and the Cliftons!' she says, confirming the town's collective attitude and ultimate judgement, evidence be damned.

'What are the Sandersons like now?' I ask.

Maeve grimaces. 'What can I say? Rubie is like a cardboard cut-out of a person. Doesn't trust anyone, not even her own shadow. And Scarlet hasn't uttered a word since, apparently. Whether it's physical or psychological, nobody knows. Either way, she's as silent as the grave.'

I shiver, picturing Scarlet now, frozen in time, locked inside her own body, her own mind. What does she think about? Can she think?

'There was another one, you know?' she says, after a pause.

'Another victim?' I ask, surprised. Mason didn't mention this.

'No, another sister. Quiet, bookish thing. Complete opposite to Rubie and Scarlet despite them being triplets.'

'Triplets?' I repeat, eyebrows raised. Mason didn't disclose that the Sanderson sisters were triplets either, despite all the research he claimed he did.

'Hmm.' Maeve nods. 'But Rosalie was always the odd one out, both in looks and personality. She never fit in with them, poor girl. In the end, she stopped trying to. Cut all her long black hair off. Dressed in dowdy, shapeless clothes. Really withdrew into herself. And then one day – poof! She just disappeared. Some – including their Uncle Silas – said she ran off with a secret boyfriend. Others thought Rubie and Scarlet's attacker had abducted her, wanted a hat trick so to speak, but she was never found. Others thought she blamed herself for what happened to her sisters and the guilt made her flee.'

'Blamed herself – why would she?' I ask, unable to hide the incredulity in my voice.

'Well, if she'd gone to that party with Rubie and Scarlet, the three of them would have walked home together and they might have made it back unscathed. Or she could have talked them out of going in the first place, what with her being the sensible one.' Maeve shrugs. 'We'll never know. But one thing I do know is that her mother died of a broken heart when she left.'

'Mason said it was a brain haemorrhage,' I state. 'And that Rosalie wrote her mother a letter a few months later to let her know she was okay.'

Maeve purses her lips. 'Anyone can write a letter,' she says. 'No proof it was from Rosalie herself. Silas was never fully convinced either. Anyway, funnily enough, just this morning a man was in here asking about her, about Rosalie. I got the impression he was an old friend.' She gives me a knowing look.

My pulse quickens. 'Really?'

'Yes. Tall, bit older, skinny, bit of an intense air about him. He's staying at Marla's, same as you. Small world, isn't it?' She chuckles.

Curiosity gets the better of me. 'Did he say why he was looking for her?'

'Not to me, no. He just bought a card and went on his way.'

I force a smile. 'Small world indeed.'

I make an excuse about needing to start typing up my notes and head for the door, my energy depleted after being in Maeve's presence and bombarded with so much information. My writer's mind races as I step back outside, trying to fill in plot holes. Who is the man looking for Rosalie after all this time? And more importantly, why her, when the main characters in the story are Rubie and Scarlet?

My reflection in the shop window catches my eyes. My pink wig, my aesthetically enhanced features, and my carefully applied make-up are all a mask, one I've perfected over the years. One that protects me. I think of Rubie Sanderson, about how her face is altered in a different way to mine and know for sure that I wouldn't want to swap places with her, or Scarlet, for a million pounds.

CHAPTER FIFTEEN

RUBIE

Rubie stands at her bedroom window watching the man wearing a dark jacket and a beanie hat approach the house. She parts the net curtains just enough to observe him without being seen herself. He strides determinedly towards the front door, like he's on a mission, but nobody ever comes here on purpose anymore, except for Dot, who's getting paid to. Their house has a way of repelling visitors, not welcoming them.

Her pulse quickens as he reaches the porch and raises a hand to grab the old brass horsehead knocker. There's something familiar about him but without seeing his face properly, she can't quite place it. Yet the way he holds himself stirs an old memory, an old feeling.

Her thoughts are interrupted by the sound of stomping along the gravel driveway. Silas is back, with his sights and his pointed finger trained on the trespasser. His face is flushed, and not just from the cold. Rubie's stomach churns. She already knows how this is going to play out. Silas doesn't handle surprises well, especially when he's been drinking. He doesn't handle anything well when he's been drinking.

'Whaddya want?' he barks, his words slurred but his aggressive attitude clear. 'Whaddever you're selling, I'm not buying. Sling yer 'ook!'

The stranger, who had immediately turned to face Silas, now raises his hands in a gesture of peace. Rubie opens the window a notch to hear their conversation better, hoping the sound or the breeze doesn't wake Scarlet who is curled up in her bed across their shared room. The dogs are lying close by, as yet oblivious to the scene unfolding outside.

'I'm sorry to turn up unannounced,' the man says. 'I'm here...' he pauses, seemingly searching for the right words.

'You a journo?' asks Silas gruffly. 'You sniffing around my nieces? 'Cos if you are, you can—'

'I'm not a journalist,' says the visitor, slicing into Silas's words. 'I'm actually here looking for Rosalie Sanderson. I was hoping that—'

Now it's Silas's turn to interrupt. 'That girl is dead to me! Dead!' His voice is loaded with anger. 'She abandoned this family, and we haven't heard from her since. Don't you dare speak her name to me, boy!' His dense dirty-grey beard quivers as he spits the words out with the depth of hatred that Rubie knows only too well. But she's on her uncle's side for once. It's the only thing they're in agreement about – Rosalie is dead to her too.

Silas steps closer, his large, lumbering frame looming over the smaller, leaner stranger, but the younger man doesn't back down. From her vantage point, Rubie gets a better view of his face, of the tension in his jaw, and she gasps in astonishment.

The visitor pulls an envelope from his bag and holds it up. 'I wanted to leave her this. Just in case she ever visits or perhaps you've got a forwarding address—'

'I said she's dead!' Silas roars, slapping the envelope out of the man's hand and onto the ground before bringing his muddy boot down on top of it as though grounding out a cigarette. He stumbles backwards awkwardly and Rubie leans forward, anticipating his fall. Unfortunately, to her disappointment, he manages to right himself virtually straight away.

The man looks up, briefly scanning the upper windows of the house as if searching for Rosalie herself and for a split-second, Rubie thinks his gaze locks onto hers through the slit in the net curtain. She jerks back from the window, her breath catching in her dry throat. Can it really be him? Surely not. He's too small, too weak-looking.

'That's right, on yer way! And don't darken this door again!' Rubie hears Silas shout, and she can't resist peering outside again. The visitor turns to leave, his head down in defeat.

Moments later the front door slams, disturbing the dogs, and the whole rickety house seems to shake with the impact. Rubie remains by the window, waiting until the stranger is completely out of sight before daring to move, while audibly tracking her uncle's movements inside the house. She hears his heavy footsteps return from the kitchen, the unmistakeable sound of a ring pull cracking open, and then the TV blaring to life in the living room. She can clearly picture him in there, slumped in her mum's old favourite floral armchair, can of beer in hand.

Once she's sure her uncle is settled for the foreseeable future, Rubie settles Oak and Elm and orders them to stay before she creeps downstairs and slips out of the front door. She hesitates for a split-second before picking the crumpled envelope up from the gravelled drive, the dirty imprint of Silas's boot on its surface, framing just one word: *Rosalie*.

Sneaking back inside, she rushes to the kitchen and sits down at the table. Ripping open the envelope, she pulls out the card inside. It looks like it has been plucked from Maeve's stock of old-fashioned cards at the post office. The front bears a raised image of a bouquet of red roses, but there are no words accompanying it. Could this man have been at the post office just before or after her this morning? A part of her wishes they'd crossed paths then, yet the thought of coming face to face with an outsider, however familiar he seems, makes her instantly cringe. It's bad enough being subjected to Maeve's close weekly scrutiny.

The short, handwritten message inside the card reads:

> Rosalie,
> I came back to tell you I'm sorry. Please forgive me.
> Fenix

It's a name she's never heard before, and there's a phone number added underneath. She must have been mistaken about who she thought the stranger was, her imagination playing tricks on her, unless he was delivering this card on this Fenix's behalf? But who is he and how does he know Rosalie – could he be the secret boyfriend Silas is convinced she had? Rubie scans the words again and again, her mind racing. All this has stirred up thoughts and feelings she's worked so hard to firstly suppress and then to make sense of. It's been challenging, a different kind of struggle to the one she faced after initially seeing her disfigured reflection in the hospital.

Her hands tremble as she folds the card and stows it in her cardigan pocket. Then she rips the envelope into many tiny pieces before throwing them in the bin, in between Silas's empty cans that Dot frequently and dutifully collects from around the house during her shifts.

The house feels stifling and oppressive. Needing to get out, Rubie grabs her coat from the hook by the back door and heads outside. She begins walking, unsure of her direction, welcoming the cold October chill.

A while later she finds herself at the beach, which is deserted except for a few seagulls squawking overhead. Rubie walks slowly along the shore, the wet sand soft and shifting beneath her shoes, and listens to the splash and crash of the waves, as restless as her mind. For a moment she imagines wading into the water, just putting one foot in front of the other, letting it steadily overwhelm her then consume her. A smooth, silent escape.

But no matter how far she walks, she can't escape the memories that are flooding back. Memories of being sixteen again, of Kayleigh's party, of Felton Clifton's mouth on hers, his hands on her body, and then... No, no she can't bear to think about it. She forces her brain to switch to something else and as usual, it turns down a familiar dark alley, the darkest alley of her life. The terror, the blood, the pain of the attack. The helplessness. The horrifying abyss that followed.

She often wishes she had died that night, for several reasons, and she has considered ending her life many times since. But she can never seem to do it. Scarlet needs her. As damaged and restrained as Rubie feels, her sister is truly broken, a fragile little caged bird who will never fly free.

The wind picks up again, whipping Rubie's hair across her face and she wraps her arms around her body for warmth. Through her thin coat, she feels the outline of the card in her cardigan pocket. *Fenix.* The name feels strange yet recognisable at the same time. Who is he and why does he care about Rosalie after all these years? And why had he looked so familiar? So much like Felton Clifton.

The thought hits her like a slap. Could this Fenix be related to him in some way? Is he here with a message from Felton? Did he get their names confused and mean to ask for her instead of Rosalie? Her heart races at the thought.

As she walks back along the beach, her mind whirls with questions, some unsettling, but most confusing. Should she bury the card deep in the bin when she gets back to the house, try to erase its existence completely... or can she harness the courage to contact this Fenix and demand to know why he's here?

SUNDAY 29TH OCTOBER 2017

CHAPTER SIXTEEN

ALLIE

I wake with a jolt, disorientated for a second as I blearily scan the gloomy room. I roll over, trying to dislodge the grogginess. The unfamiliar weight of the duvet and bedspread keeps me moulded to the mattress, but I know I won't be able to fall back to sleep now, not after such a restless night. For some reason, I kept hearing a baby crying. It must have been the B&B's neighbour or perhaps an exhausted mother up at dawn to walk her child in its pram along the prom. Like Marla said, the sea air can work wonders. But still, the sound haunted me, scraping my nerves and disturbing my sleep.

A thin slice of morning light squeezes through the gap in the middle of the heavy curtains, dust motes floating in the air. I sit up and run my hands through my thin, natural hair. My pink wig sits on top of the dressing table and a few of its candyfloss-coloured strands catch the light prettily.

I reach for my phone and check the time – 8.11am. Too early for a Sunday but I need to get up, get on with the day. And I'm already counting down the hours until tonight and my second visit to Mason's house. His invitation still lingers in my mind, causing a reaction in me I haven't felt in a while, especially for a man. Although I'm not normally a fan of surprises in life, this instant attraction to Mason is quite a pleasant one.

Throwing back the duvet I get up and stretch, raising my arms high above my head before dropping down to touch my toes. Under the threadbare carpet the floorboards creak as I cross to the window and pull back the curtains. The view remains unchanged: the desolate prom, the slate-grey sky and the wide, wide expanse of choppy sea. Stonethorpe looks lifeless and all I've got to keep me company are shadowy thoughts that have formed from my conversations with locals so far. The Sanderson case, the Cliftons, the fair, Rosalie... it all twists together into one messy knot I'm not sure I'm equipped to untangle into a couple of easy-to-read chapters.

I lean my forehead against the cool glass and remind myself yet again that I'm not here to solve a mystery. This isn't an investigation. I'm a ghostwriter not a detective, and I just need to stick to the facts as they're presented to me and maybe embellish them with some scenic descriptions. Ralph is paying me well, but not enough to chase and catch old ghosts.

Yet the more I learn, the harder it is not to get sucked in, despite not wanting to. There's just something *off* about Stonethorpe-On-Sea; it's got a weird vibe, and not just because of the Sanderson case.

I push myself off the window and make my way to the en suite. I'm meeting the Roberts family today, the couple who own and still live next to the land where the fair used to pitch, and I need to get ready.

The old Sandy Crest Caravan Park site is even more depressing than I expected. Like a patch of desert, it's mostly barren with tufts of weeds and a few dead bushes dotting its surface. A large iron gate, once painted white, still stands pointlessly at its entrance given there are no other perimeter markers whatsoever. I step out of my car and scan the empty field once more before pulling out my phone and taking a few photos. Then I head towards the bungalow next door.

Caroline Roberts greets me cheerfully at the door. I know from Ebony's research that she and her husband Phillip are only in their forties – her early and him late – but they both look much older. Caroline treats me like I'm a celebrity, super smiley and welcoming, her thick, greying hair swept back into a neat bun. Phillip, on the other hand, hangs back, his hands shoved deep into his trouser pockets, his blank expression harder to read than his closed-off body language.

'Come on through,' says Caroline brightly, leading me through to a warm and well-presented, albeit dated, living room. Phillip trails silently behind me. There's a strong floral smell, as though air freshener has just been sprayed, and I find it strangely comforting, a throwback to my childhood. My mum loved florals.

'Thanks for agreeing to talk to me,' I say, as Caroline invites me to take a seat on the settee. She sits in the armchair opposite and gestures for Phillip to pour the drinks from the teapot already placed on the coffee table between us. Mugs, sugar and milk have already been laid out too. He obliges dutifully as Caroline settles back.

'No problem at all,' she says in response. 'We don't get many visitors these days so it's nice to have some company.'

I take in the room while Phillip distributes our cups of tea. The walls contain many framed family photos and canvases, mostly of two identical girls. Their faces stare down at me eerily. Twins have always freaked me out, as though they're one person split into two. Half the personality, half the brain cells.

'Hazel and Olive,' Caroline says proudly, noticing me scanning the pictures. 'They're sixteen now – time flies!'

'Sixteen and a handful,' Phillip adds quietly, finally taking a seat himself. It's the first time he's spoken since I arrived.

I smile politely but his comment makes me shiver, remembering the Sanderson girls were just sixteen too. I take out my list of questions and phone and ask their permission to record the interview.

'Is that necessary?' asks Phillip. I regard him curiously. Why is he so cagey?

'No, but it will ensure greater accuracy for the book, and I can anonymise names if you'd prefer?'

He appears to think about it for a few seconds and then gives a barely imperceptible nod. I press the button and begin.

'I understand you both grew up here in Stonethorpe, right? You must have seen a lot of changes over the years.'

Caroline nods. 'Yes, we've been here for it all. Before the fair and after. We thought about leaving after... you know... but then a couple of years later I fell pregnant with the girls. And with family ties here, we decided to stay on, didn't we, Phillip?'

Her husband glances at her, his expression still tight. He nods too.

'Did you ever go to the Halloween fair yourselves,' I ask, determined to stay on track, inviting them to talk more about the fair itself rather than all the scandals and crimes seemingly associated with it.

'We did. I still remember the first year it was ever here. Oh, the excitement!' Caroline claps her hands together. 'I've never been one for the big, scary rides but I loved all the prize stalls. And as for the atmosphere – it was electric back in the day. Nothing but fun. We'd go two or three times during fair week in the beginning, before the prices got sky high. One pound for a spin on the waltzers, can you believe it? Of course, that doesn't sound like much now but—'

Phillip coughs loudly, interrupting her.

Caroline's smile falters. 'Sorry,' she says to me. 'I forget myself sometimes.'

It's a strange expression and one which seems to come easily after a not-so-subtle signal from her husband. If he doesn't let her speak about something as simple as ride prices, I'm not going to get much out of them. I need to be more direct. I check my list of questions again and skip a few of the warm-up ones.

'When was the last time you went to the fair?' I ask.

'1997,' says Caroline straight away. 'We were both there that night. The night that everything changed.'

She doesn't look at her husband and she doesn't have to specify what night. I know she means the night of the attack on Rubie and Scarlet Sanderson.

Phillip shifts in his seat. 'It was a long time ago,' he mutters. 'And those sisters weren't even there; they were at that party.'

I'm grateful that for once someone is severing the Sandersons from the fair. This is more like it – someone willing to consider them separate events rather than lumping them all together like everyone else has.

Caroline doesn't respond, just looks down at her hands, twisting her wedding ring around her finger. Phillip stares at the teacup in front of him, still untouched.

The ongoing tension makes me feel uncomfortable, so I sip my tepid tea, which is too weak for my tastes, mentally considering my next question. Clearly Caroline is more comfortable talking to me than Phillip, but I suspect what he's got to say could be much more interesting. Not that he seems willing to share. He's a very guarded man, seemingly here to oversee his rambling wife.

Caroline breaks the taut silence. Her voice is soft, sad.

'There was more going on that night. Things that people don't talk about. Pranks, supposedly.' She shrugs and Phillip shoots her a warning look.

But now I'm intrigued. Maybe she can be interesting, after all.

'Pranks?' I ask.

A few more moments of silence pass. I can feel myself getting impatient but the power of not speaking first is potent. Caroline flicks an anxious glance in her husband's direction, a silent communication. He sighs, rolls his eyes to the artexed ceiling.

He plants his hands on his thighs as though fortifying himself and nods once, decision made. Here it comes, whatever he's been keeping contained. 'Me and the Clifton boys... we... we messed about a bit back then, especially during fair week with the fair workers. Harmless fun, mostly. But that night, well, things got out of hand. At that party after the fair.'

Caroline begins wringing her hands, her mouth set in a thin line. I didn't expect anything like this and Phillip's candour has caught me off guard. His voice is raw. My resolve to not dig too deeply is out the window. I want to know what he's going to say.

'We were just kids, remember. Everyone makes mistakes when they're young. But that night, well it changed everything. The dares went too far.' He hangs his head, his bald patch visible.

Caroline nods fervently. 'Phillip stopped hanging round with them after that – those Clifton boys. We settled down and got engaged and he started working full time for his father. He had absolutely nothing to do with what happened in 1998!'

The unsaid implication being that he might have had something to do with what happened in 1997 though? I feel a bit sick as I gaze at him, this spindly, balding man. It's clear there's now even more to the story and while I'm not here to solve a cold case, it's impossible to not make deductions and assumptions. I can see it in the way they avoid each other's eyes, and the way Phillip's gruff voice catches when he talks about the past.

'Anyway, the town hasn't been the same since,' says Caroline. Her hand trembles as she puts down her teacup. 'But it's a lot safer for our girls now.'

I wonder if that's really true but don't comment.

'You said you had family ties here. Would they be open to talking to me about their memories of the fair?' I ask Phillip.

Caroline answers for him. 'Phillip's father passed away a few years ago.' She sighs, her expression hardening. 'But even if he was still around, I doubt he'd have agreed to a chat. Man of very few words was my father-in-law.'

If looks could kill, Caroline would be stone dead in her chair judging by Phillip's dark, narrowed eyes. His jaw tightens and I get the impression she's tactfully glossing over her true feelings. I decide to push it, out of devilment more than anything, to make Phillip feel as uncomfortable as I've felt while being here.

'Strong and silent type, was he?'

Caroline's laugh is sharp. 'Ha! That's one way to put it. We've nearly split up a few times over the years because of him, haven't we, Phil?' Phillip deigns to grunt in response before turning his head towards the window, looking out on the sparse expanse of land next to the house. I wonder what old scenes play out for him. 'Yet he always had some scheme, some plan hatching,' Caroline continues. 'Him and Clifton Snr. were two peas in a pod. They way they looked down their noses at people... and the way they looked at young girls, including me, well, it gave me the creeps.'

'That's enough, Carol,' says Phillip.

The air feels heavy again, charged with something

unspoken. I gulp another mouthful of tea, both drawn to ask more questions yet desperate to leave.

'So, what happened at the party after the fair?' I ask boldly. Suddenly, I want to know.

'Are you really writing a book about the town fair?' he asks, pinioning me with a suspicious glare.

'Yes,' I reply.

'It seems to me you're asking an awful lot of unrelated questions. How do we know you're not a journalist here to try to dig up old dirt?'

'Phillip...' whispers Caroline.

'No, Carol, I'm not having it. She's trying to drag us back there!'

'I'm really not,' I protest. I try not to flinch as I hold his gaze. 'I'm just trying to gather information for the book I've been commissioned to write,' I say, making a point of reminding them that I'm merely the middle woman here. But their reaction – Phillip's in particular – has intrigued me. Why agree to me visiting their home to chat about the fair if it's such a touchy subject for them? Or maybe I'm reading them all wrong and the history I get the distinct impression they're trying to swerve is more personal than public. Infidelity perhaps? Criminal behaviour disguised as the pranks they mentioned? Either way, I'm glad when Caroline intervenes, sounding firmer this time.

'I think we'll leave it there now, if you don't mind, Allie. It's ancient history and we've all moved on.'

Her obvious lie hangs in the air but their closed-up expressions speak for themselves. It's time for me to leave.

'I'll show you out,' she says, already halfway to the door. I chance another glance at Phillip as I stow my notebook and phone in my bag but he has already moved to the window, looking out again with his hands shoved in both pockets.

As I leave their bungalow and head back to the car, I rake

back over the meeting. Phillip's caginess. Caroline's bitterness. Their connections to the fair through Phillip's friendship with the Colton boys and his father's alliance with Mr Sandy Crest himself. Does Mason know all this too? I make a mental note to ask him tonight if he knows how these disparate parts of the puzzle fit together, acknowledging that despite my best efforts, I've definitely become sucked into Stonethorpe's dark past. And the more I find out, the more complicated it seems.

CHAPTER SEVENTEEN

FENIX

Fenix has lain awake for a while. The heaviness in his chest feels suffocating; disappointment mixed with frustration. Yesterday's visit to the Sanderson house replays in his head on a loop. Silas Sanderson storming towards him, his blotchy, bloated, bearded face twisted in rage. *That girl is dead to me!* He can still hear the man's depressing declaration about Rosalie ringing in his ears.

Fenix rubs his hands over his head and face, trying to scrub away the helpless feeling, wondering what to do next. This trip is already taking more of a toll on him than he anticipated, and he thinks of what Janelle said: *You can just come home, you know.* But he knows he can't, not yet. He goes into himself, imagines being back on the gravel driveway with hope still in his heart. He just wanted to find her or at least find a way to contact her.

With a gasp he sits up, his mind snagging on something. Or rather someone. A figure up at the window shrouded by the net curtain. Was it Rosalie watching him from above? Or could it have been one of her sisters – Rubie or Scarlet? He vividly recalls Rosalie telling him their mum had given them all "red" names, back when she wanted to willingly share details about herself with him, before he showed himself as a monster.

Now his mind is racing. What if Rosalie has been living there all along and the whole runaway story is just a smokescreen? Could she have been hiding in that house for all these years, with Silas performing the role of fierce guard dog in the guise of a domineering, drunken uncle? Fenix shakes his head, perplexed by the possibility. Did Rosalie need that much protection after her sisters' attack? Either way, whether she stayed or fled, he needs to make amends somehow, to assuage his guilt before it's too late.

He gets out of bed and pads to the en-suite bathroom. He begins his morning routine, going through the automatic physical motions of washing and dressing. He doesn't dwell too long on his haggard reflection in the tarnished mirror, preferring to let his subconscious tick, tick, tick. It's not long before his mind drifts back to the past...

It had started innocently enough. A crush on a pretty girl who tilted her head in the cutest way when she listened to him, like he had something worthwhile to say. A dangerous desire he hadn't been able to control. But it wasn't just lust, a basic primal urge like all those other times, this was something more, something special, something pure. Just like her. He had followed her, watched her for a while and his obsession had quickly grown. Then one day, one beautiful but blustery summer's day, he got lucky and got chatting to her, on the dunes behind where the Halloween fair pitched. She was sad that day, but he managed to make her smile, and the weeks that followed were magical, some of the best of his life back then. Their conversations had been oxygen for him, allowing him to escape the suffocating rigidity of his home life. She made him forget about the pain of his parents' divorce, his dad's military grade rules and punishments, his older brother's taboo desires...

Although that wasn't the whole truth, and it took a long time to admit that to himself. He'd always had a dark side, a part of him that thrived whenever he walked the tightrope of cruelty and recklessness. It was embedded in him. For a while, being around Rosalie made him think he could successfully harness it and lock it away inside himself for ever, but it only got worse, demanding to be let out. You can't contain chaos.

Dressed now, Fenix throws back his cocktail of tablets and washes them down with half a glass of water. He pulls on his jacket and his beanie hat then slips out of his room, makes his way down through the hall and outside, quietly pulling the B&B's door closed behind him, thankful to have not run into Marla. He's in no mood for idle small talk this morning; he's got too much on his mind.

The cold air nips at his skin but he barely notices as he begins to pound the pavement, his feet taking him onwards, his vision blinkered.

When he arrives at his destination, the old site is a desolate wasteland, the dunes just beyond a graveyard of memories. The weeds have overtaken where the fairground used to stand, popping up every year at the end of October, brought to life by the fair worker's hands and nuts and bolts and electric cables as thick as snakes. He enjoyed watching them as they moved as though choreographed. He was fascinated by their accents and envious of their easy, coarse laughter. Then they recruited him, his brother and their mates, and brought them into their fold. He felt proud and powerful and part of things. He recalls the wicked things they all used to do, first to the tourists when they swarmed in and then to the locals too. He remembers the cruel jokes they'd played on the kids, minimising them as "pranks", the way they terrorised and humiliated anyone they deemed weak or pathetic. They'd thrived on it back then, enjoyed the power they felt, the hollow, demonic laughs they shared. Now he's just ashamed. Ashamed of who he was and what he did, to them all.

He stands still for a while next to the lone iron gate, occasionally wincing as more memories fling themselves forward, gasping for air after finally being freed from imprisonment. His breath has thinned to shallow gasps, and he places a palm to his chest, trying to regulate himself. The guilt that's been gnawing at him for decades has even sharper teeth and is taking bigger bites of him now he's back here. The full extent of what he did is now playing in his brain like a high-definition psychological thriller movie.

He catches movement in his peripheral vision and turns his head to the left. A woman walks briskly to a car parked outside the nearby bungalow. Her hair is pink, the same shade as the candyfloss that was sold at the fair. He realises she must be the writer Marla mentioned, the other guest at the B&B. Marla had joked about him being on his best behaviour or else he might end up in her book. He keeps his head down but watches her surreptitiously – old habits die hard – and finds himself assessing her favourably. She's petite, extremely attractive, has a determined air about her, a gold necklace around her neck. He feels drawn to her.

What if he told her his story? Purged it all – the guilt, the shame, his catalogue of sins – to someone who could articulate his regret, his apologies much better than he can. Maybe confessing would be like shedding his old skin, cleansing his conscience, leaving an honest account for his daughter to read one day so she'll understand how sorry he is, how he wishes so desperately he could go back in time and undo it all.

Fenix continues to watch as the woman gets into her car and drives away. He toys with the idea of returning to the B&B, knocking on the door to her room and asking to speak to her. Informing her he has some untold background for her book, if she wants it. As soon as he thinks it, the doubt creeps in. Would telling her really absolve him of what he's done, or would it cause fresh heartache for those he hurt and those he now loves? Does he really want his legacy to be a chapter of a random book? No, better not to tell an outsider anything. And there's only one person whose forgiveness he truly craves anyway. Maybe he'll try again. Maybe he'll go back to the Sanderson house and refuse to leave until he's got answers. Maybe Rosalie herself will open the door next time. Maybe she'll listen to him. Maybe, just maybe, he'll finally find the peace he craves more than anything.

31ST OCTOBER 1996
SCARLET

Today I finally turned sweet sixteen! I'm writing this in bed at nine o'clock at night as we've just got back from the Halloween fair! I've been waiting for today for so long and tonight was the best night of my life. The fair was spooky and magical and loads of people were dressed up, but me and Rubie wore our new Morgan jeans that Mum gave us for our birthday. (Rosalie got books – how boring! Rubie mocked her all day, obviously.)

The very best part of the fair was that the gorgeous boy who operates the waltzers gave me and Rubie a free go! He saw we were wearing our birthday badges, and he winked and smiled at me when we were waiting for the ride to start! (Rubie said he was looking at her, but he wasn't, I'm sure of it.)

Later, another boy who was in charge of the ghost train flirted with us too. He said he liked twins and asked us if we wanted a threesome! I wasn't sure what he meant but as quick as a flash Rubie said she didn't like to share and he laughed. I giggled too but she told him I didn't even know what a threesome was in that nasty way of hers. Is it like being a triplet? She always tries to make me look stupid, especially in front of boys.

Mum said we had to be home by eight o'clock, so we rode our bikes there and back to save time walking. Even that bit was fun! Mum's friend Mrs Roberts let us store our bikes in one of the empty Sandy Crest caravans next to her house, so they didn't get stolen. I'm glad Mr Roberts wasn't there when we collected them because he's well creepy. Rubie said he "undressed her with his eyes", which sounds gross and weird, but she was probably trying to make me feel stupid then too. I mean how can you undress someone with your eyes?

Anyway, apart from Rubie being a bit of a bitch at times, it was a totally dreamy night. I even heard my faves Take That being played while we were on one of the rides! I'm already excited to go again next year! (Maybe by then I'll know what a threesome is or maybe Rubie might have had a personality transplant and finally be a nice person!)

SUNDAY 29TH OCTOBER 2017

CHAPTER EIGHTEEN

ALLIE

'Right on time,' says Mason, sweeping an arm wide to welcome me into his home for the second time in two days. I smile as I smooth down a few flyaway strands of my wig; the short walk from the car to the door was blustery to say the least. It feels like a storm is on its way. Tonight's alter ego is the cool blonde. Why not? I like to mix it up a bit and Mason's appreciative once-over gives me the tingles. It's a promising start to the night.

Mason's house is warm and cosy and again filled with a pleasant, masculine scent. I inhale as he takes my coat; he smells good too.

'So, ready for those articles?' he asks, and I'm momentarily stunned. Is he just going to hand them to me and that's it, send me on my way again? Has he changed his mind about us spending the evening together?

My question is answered as we enter the kitchen. Two full glasses of red wine sit on the table next to copies of all the newspaper stories he showed me yesterday. Soft music curls around me and Mason smiles as he folds my coat over the back of one of the stools at the island.

'I do like an organised man,' I say as he invites me to sit. I do and immediately begin scanning all the printed copies. There are more of them today.

'I thought I'd dig out everything I had. Some of the more recent ones are just filler pieces but you're welcome to them all.' He moves a few of them closer to me and as I reach out for them his fingers brush against mine, lingering for a second. There's that stomach flip again.

I flick through the clippings briefly, skimming the headlines. The front-page stories include photos too, mostly of sixteen-year-old Rubie and Scarlet, mirror images of each other and smiling for the camera. The photos remind me of another set of twins – Hazel and Olive Roberts – which in turn reminds me about today's interview with their parents.

'I had an interesting conversation with Caroline and Phillip Roberts today, as you suggested,' I tell him before taking a sip of wine. It's rich and delicious.

'Oh yes?' He sits next to me, clearly eager for the update.

'Well, I say conversation, but it was fairly one-sided. They actually got really cagey at one point, especially the husband. He definitely didn't want me there.'

'Really? What did he say?' asks Mason.

I frown. 'Well, it was what Caroline said that started it off, I think. She told me that Phillip used to hang around with the Colton boys and the fair workers. Apparently, they played a lot of pranks, as they called them, but she stated that he definitely didn't have anything to do with what happened in 1998.'

Mason lifts his eyebrows. 'But what about what happened in 1997?'

'Exactly what I thought!' I exclaim. 'It's weird that she specified just one of the years, isn't it? She also claimed that Phillip's father and Clifton Snr. were as thick as thieves and not exactly nice men. Were they interviewed by the police after the attacks?'

Mason nods, swallowing his mouthful of wine. 'All the local men were interviewed. They even brought in a few extra officers from a neighbouring force to conduct them. There obviously wasn't enough evidence to formally arrest anyone, let alone charge them.'

'Well, Phillip Roberts seemed shady to me. Accused me of being a journalist too.'

'How insulting,' says Mason, his tone deadpan.

'The worst,' I retort. He smiles first.

I take another sip of wine and relax into my chair. 'So, who do you think attacked Rubie and Scarlet?' I ask.

Mason tilts his head, considering the question. Judging by his extensive body of work, he must have asked himself the question a thousand times.

'I reckon it was Silas Sanderson,' he states definitively. 'The guy's a wreck. Drinks himself into oblivion most nights yet he remains in that house with those girls... women now,' he corrects himself. 'I think that's a sign of guilt eating him alive. He's either trying to atone somehow, by watching over them in his own way, or he gets some sort of sick satisfaction by sitting ringside and revelling in the effects of his handiwork day in, day out.'

'That's really dark,' I say.

He shrugs. 'Or else he did it for the money. He inherited the farmhouse and all of his sister's money, which was a sizeable sum, so they say. She lived frugally for years after her husband died in order to provide for her girls.'

'Interesting theories,' I say. 'Could he have killed her too?'

He shrugs but his eyes are intense, glistening. This is obviously his *Mastermind* subject; he loves talking about it. 'Maybe not directly, but an ailing parent is only going to get worse coping with not only two of her daughters being attacked and left for dead, but the third going missing soon after.'

'Yes, what about the runaway sister? What if she holds the key to all of it?' I ask.

Mason sighs heavily. 'Well, that's another layer to the mystery, isn't it? That secret boyfriend story never sat right with me, but again, an absence of evidence equals no evidence. Maybe she's still out there somewhere.'

He leans closer, his breath sweet from the wine. 'But what about you, Allie? You're the outsider here. No history in Stonethorpe. No biases. From what you've discovered so far, what do you think happened to the Sanderson sisters? What is your gut telling you?'

My gut is telling me it's time to stop talking. I don't actually want to dig that deeply. I don't actually care what happened to those girls, not really.

Instead of answering, I close the space between us and press my lips to his. He welcomes it, instantly responding, kissing me deeply, urgently. He's rough in a way that excites me, and I lose myself in the moment, pulling him up and wrapping my arms around his neck, raking my fingers through his hair. He pushes me backwards against the edge of the island, lifts me up onto it, and I let him. No more thoughts of cold cases or mysteries or fairgrounds whatsoever. Just this, now.

The next morning, I wake up in Mason's bed. He's still asleep beside me, his breathing slow and steady. I must have worn him out. Stealthily, I slip out from under the duvet and gather my underwear up from the floor before creeping downstairs to collect the rest of my clothes. Last night was a lot of fun but today I need my own space again.

Grabbing the pile of copied articles I ostensibly came here for, I head through the hallway to the front door. On my way, I notice a photo of a little girl. Her front two teeth are missing but her smile is Cheshire cat-like. She has Mason's eyes. I remember being that young and happy, before my dad died and everything changed. So many sad, separate life events can really change someone irrevocably. A sound from upstairs jolts me out of my maudlin thoughts, but instead of waiting to see if it means Mason's awake and on his way downstairs, I unlock the door and hurry out.

I drive back to the B&B with the window down, enjoying the sharp tang of the sea air and the feeling of the breeze through my now dishevelled wig. It's itchy and I can't wait to take it off and scrub at my scalp with my fingernails.

I keep my hood up as I enter the grand terraced property, peering around the door to check the coast is clear. But as I walk through the entrance hallway towards the stairs clutching the folder of Mason's articles, I spot Rye cleaning in the front lounge. I stop in the doorway, pleased to see him.

'Helping mummy with the housekeeping?' I can't help but joke, a smirk on my lips.

I expect a quick quip in return or at least a grin, but he looks away. 'Yeah, something like that.' I detect an awkwardness in the air but before I can say anything more, Marla bustles in from the back of the house.

'Hello there, Allie dear.' She openly appraises me as she dries her hands on her pinny. 'Just coming in or just going out?' she asks.

I'm about to tell her it's none of her business when Rye squeezes between us and off down the hallway.

'All done, son?' she calls after him.

'Yeah,' he replies without even turning back.

She pats my arm. 'Don't mind him. He's always been a bit of an enigma. Ever since we got him,' she says before moving into the dining room.

Got him? What a strange way to phrase it. Maybe she's one

of those bonkers people who still believe the stork brings babies, the Easter Bunny brings chocolate eggs and Father Christmas brings presents.

Regardless, I don't have the energy to give it any extra thought. I need to take my wig off, have a hot shower and then get on with some work before it's time to leave. I hurry up the stairs, eager to get to my room, but as I unlock the door and step inside, a strange feeling grips me. I sense a glitch in the matrix.

I survey my surroundings. My wheelie case is still lying on the floor, zipped up as I left it. My hoodie is still hanging off the back of the dressing-table chair and my laptop is closed on top of the dressing table, unmoved. Fresh towels have been delivered again and placed on the bed – not that I was expecting any due to leaving today.

But that's when I notice it. My photo of the girl and the baby. Instead of being stuck to the middle of the mirror where I left it, the photo is now face down next to my laptop. Someone's moved it.

I close the door behind me, throw the folder of articles on the bed, and put the picture back. I slide my phone out of my pocket to distract me and divert the disquietness and as I do, a message flashes up on its screen. I wonder if it might be from Mason but hope it isn't. Eager men texting too soon is another item for my hate list. However, when I see the short message is from Claudia, I take it back. An eager man is preferable to the bitter reminder that the woman I still love doesn't want me anymore. I roll my eyes and toss the phone onto the bed too. My ex-girlfriend's timing is impeccable, as always. She can wait for a reply.

After my shower, I take my time drying my hair, trying to disguise as many scalp patches as possible. I've attempted to train it into that many different directions over the years, it's no wonder it doesn't want to do as it's told anymore. Still, it doesn't really matter as I never go out in public without wearing a wig, but I live in hope that one day either my hair will grow back fully or that I just won't give a fuck anymore. I suspect the latter is more likely.

Talking of not giving a fuck, my phone rings and I'm childishly amused that it's Claudia. I haven't responded to her snippy message yet and she hates being ignored. Well, tough. If she thinks I'm going to move out even sooner than planned because Shelley thinks I should, she can think again. Sisters… always causing problems. I decline the call and put my phone on silent and then freeze as something catches my eye – a shadow under the door.

I hold my breath, waiting for a knock or Marla's voice, but nothing happens. No movement, no sound. I stare at the gap, waiting, wondering who's there and what they want. Questioning whether they were the one who moved my photo. Maybe it's just Rye cleaning upstairs, I tell myself, but I daren't call his name. After several tense seconds the shadow moves, and I exhale. The relief is palpable, but I know it's only temporary. One of these days the shadow that's been at my door for twenty years is finally going to break through and snatch me, extract my deepest, darkest secrets from me, and swallow me whole.

MONDAY 30TH OCTOBER 2017

CHAPTER NINETEEN

RUBIE

Rubie returns to the farmhouse with the damp chill of the sea air still clinging to her clothes and skin. Entering the small lobby through the back door, she removes her sandy boots and places them beside Scarlet's folded up wheelchair, then hangs her thin coat on one of the wall hooks. She manages a smile as she hears Oak and Elm scratching and whining at the kitchen door, desperate to see her. She opens it and lets them barrel into her. She envelops them both in her arms, kissing their velvet heads and taking comfort in their relentless loyalty and affection. She remembers, as she often does when fussing them, about how Silas wanted to drown the litter when they discovered their previous family dog was pregnant. The only reason he relented was because puppies meant more beer money so four of them were sold. Rubie successfully fought to keep Oak and Elm, and it had been the only unexpected turn of fate that had turned out happily in her whole life. They're getting old now, which makes her sad. She tries not to think about it too much or the anticipatory devastation already feels too much to bear, even when they're right here in her arms, like this.

As the dogs' avid welcome dance winds down, Rubie hears

a familiar yet annoying sound coming from the walk-in pantry. She can hear it despite Silas's snoring reverberating around the ground floor of the house. She walks across the kitchen, the dogs following closely behind. There it is again: a crunching. She pushes open the pantry door and feels her temper immediately flare at the sight before her. Scarlet is sitting cross-legged on the floor surrounded by empty cereal boxes and biscuit and cracker wrappers. The contents of all of them are crunched all around her, some still in her palms, and there are crumbs dotted around her mouth and caught in her hair. She looks up at Rubie and smiles a smile of unbridled glee.

'Not again, Scarlet!' she snaps, clicking her fingers at the dogs to keep them back, to stop them from diving into the floor buffet snouts first. She sends them to their beds and instructs them to stay before turning back to her sister, who remains oblivious to the anger and frustration surging through Rubie. 'I go out for half an hour and this is what you get up to! Help me clean this up before Uncle Silas sees what you've done!'

Scarlet's grin doesn't fade and her eyes are wide and playful, seemingly completely disconnected from reality. She's been like this for years now; broken yet childlike. Rubie knows she should have checked the pantry door was locked before she left the house, but she wishes that for once she didn't have to constantly either safeguard her sister or protect the contents of their home from her. She desperately craves more free time for herself than just the duration of Scarlet's naps and Dot's few shifts.

She shakes her head in frustration as her sister resumes squeezing biscuits in each hand. 'You're useless, Scarlet,' she mutters under her breath, her tone as bitter as her thoughts.

A grunt from behind makes Rubie jump and she spins around. Silas stands in the kitchen, a crumpled beer can in his hand. He's always had the knack for creeping up on her; she hadn't even registered that the snoring had stopped. The dogs stay in their beds, choosing to observe from afar. Rubie knows where Oak and Elm's loyalties lie, and it's not with the man who wanted to drown them at birth.

Silas flicks his bloodshot eyes between his nieces, assessing the situation. It takes him a minute, as though his brain can't process what his eyes take in straight away. 'Get that mess cleaned up,' he says although there's no real conviction to his order. He's obviously still a bit groggy.

Rubie feels a zap of injustice. 'She's your niece as well as my sister,' she states. 'Why don't you help me clean it up instead of standing there like a zombie?'

Silas launches his crushed can at Rubie and she ducks just in time. It lands on the floor and the foamy dregs inside splutter out. He takes a step forward, his face etched with fury, his fist clenched, and Rubie instinctively moves to stand in front of Scarlet, faking a show of bravado. Being petite and weakened, she's not exactly a match for her taller and stronger – albeit drunken – uncle, but she can defend herself better than her sister can. She's proved that many times over the years, even during his fitter days when he used to tend to the house and grounds. Teeth and nails can still cause decent enough damage when necessary.

'Och, it's not worth the bother, lassie,' Silas states before ambling to the fridge and retrieving another can. As he leaves the kitchen, Rubie breathes a sigh of relief. Not that she was really expecting a fight. He's been declining even more rapidly the past few years and lately he's become all mouth and no action. He's just here, taking up space in their mother's house like Lord of the Manor, like he owns the place when it's rightfully theirs. They endure his frequent rants, his disgusting stench, his vomit in the toilet and often elsewhere around the house, and for what? For the pretence of a "family"? It's a joke. The saddest joke she's ever known.

She turns back to Scarlet, her frustration abating, sympathy and pity flooding back in. 'How about a hot chocolate?' she asks. Scarlet's wide smile returns, and she nods, clapping enthusiastically.

Rubie reaches down and helps to pull her sister up. She deposits her at the kitchen table with a colouring book and pencils before making her the drink she doesn't deserve after the stunt she's just pulled. But she can't punish Scarlet for not understanding right from wrong. Well, maybe she can in a small way – she doesn't add the usual marshmallows this time and feels a perverse pleasure from withholding them.

As Rubie sets about cleaning out the pantry, she lets her mind wander and it soon stops, as it often does, at thoughts of her mum. She decides she'll visit her later, once Scarlet and Silas are asleep again.

Just before dusk, Rubie stomps across the yard. She passes the chicken coop and the now empty barn-cum-stable that used to house Maple and the rabbits, and follows the dilapidated fence to the farmhouse's side gate. Once through it, she hurries on her way.

A while later, when she reaches the graveyard, the familiar sight of her mother's headstone instantly comforts her. It's strange how a thick slab of concrete does more for her emotionally than her living, breathing uncle, and the headstone itself epitomises that. He chose the cheapest, plainest marker for her loving, beautiful mum. It bears nothing more than her name and the two dates of her birth and death. No sentimental wording, no poetry, no acknowledgement of her daughters. Rubie seethes about it frequently.

She also acknowledges that if Rosalie had still been here when their mum died, she would have suggested a meaningful inscription. She always had a way with words, being so into her books, and despite them being triplets, Rosalie always seemed like the grown-up, empathetic one. Then again, if she hadn't disappeared maybe none of this would have happened. She could have organised a home help or a nurse or something for their mum. Perhaps in some parallel universe, Rosalie could have prevented Silas from inserting himself into the family homestead under the pretence of a concerned patriarch, permanently infecting their lives with his greed, selfishness and alcohol addiction. It was easier for them all to manage him when he just visited occasionally to help with the animals and cut the hay – four wilful females against one of him, and his drinking wasn't anywhere near as bad back then. But ever since Rubie and Scarlet became such diminished versions of themselves, he has become even angrier and nastier, and therefore able to overpower them easily.

And if she's thinking about parallel universes, what about one where their beloved dad hadn't died when they were fourteen? What if that other fateful night hadn't happened, and they hadn't been attacked? What if she wasn't scarred and resentful and just a husk of the woman she could – should – have become? At just sixteen, she dreamed of a life with Felton Clifton, back when she believed in the happily-ever-after tales like the ones their mum used to read to her and Scarlet and Rosalie when their dad was still alive. In those days, their current reality would have seemed like a horrific nightmare, an exhaustive list of what they would never, ever want to happen in their lives. Instead, Rubie remembered those stories and projected her hopes for her and Felton's relationship long into the future – leaving Stonethorpe, getting married, building a life together. Teenage sweethearts for ever. Well, he wasn't a teenager at the time, but she still was, and she romanticised the idea of an enduring first love.

But that dream died a long time ago. Along with everything else. She clenches her teeth and fists, presses her nails painfully into her palms. It's not fair. She deserves better than this. Yes, she behaved bitchily when she was younger, but karma really did her dirty. The familiar wave of bitterness flows through her, strong enough that she feels it could drown her. But instead, she stands there as silent as her sister, staring at her mother's grave. Because what else can she do? She can't change the past now.

She once again thinks about the stranger who came looking for Rosalie. The memories he stirred up. The suspicions he prompted. No, she can't change the past now, but maybe she can make more sense of the present by plucking up the courage to contact the mystery visitor. Resolved to do so, she says goodbye to her mum and heads back home.

CHAPTER TWENTY

FENIX

Fenix sits in the corner of the café not far from the B&B, his narrow shoulders hunched, and his hands wrapped around his mug of black coffee. The calm space is neutral, its walls painted a soft latte colour, with open shelves bearing potted plants and framed postcards and seaside-themed trinkets. The sounds around him are comforting, a gentle white noise soundtrack while he thinks. The low chatter of the few other customers, the clinking of spoons against cups and saucers, the hiss of the coffee machine. It's warm and cosy and the pastry and coffee aromas are so comforting. He wishes he could stay here all day; pretend he's in a café near to home waiting for Janelle and Milly to join him later. But he's not there, he's here.

He glances back down at the local newspaper on his table. Yet another monotonous story about the Sanderson sisters features on its front page. He wonders if they just reprint the same articles year after year, only adding the word "still": *The case still remains unsolved.* He's grateful for the lazy journalism though, and the way the case stalled. He's thankful that nobody ever found out about his own adjacent crime, either then or since.

Fenix takes a sip of his now tepid coffee, the caffeine probably not helping his nervous system or decreasing the anxious buzz inside him ahead of today's task. After a lot of thought, he has decided to buy some flowers and return to the Sanderson house, to personally deliver a bouquet for Rosalie's birthday. Her thirty-sixth. He remembers it every year, a date as familiar to him as his wife and daughter's birthdates. He wonders if he'll see his own birthday next year, his forty-second. It'll be a miracle if he does, based on what the grave-faced doctors have been telling him this year.

He sets his mug down, his hand shaking slightly. He's tired – exhausted in a way that rest can't fix. It's a strange thing to look death in the face and he often thinks his cancer is a payback of some kind, for evading legal justice. And now, with his own mortality looming ever closer, he must do something to make it right.

He goes over the plan again: take the flowers to the farmhouse and if Rosalie isn't there then he'll have to leave them on the doorstep and go to the church. He'll finally confess his sins to the vicar and hope for absolution, even if it's from the wrong person. He's held it in for too long and now he needs to let it out.

Yet the concept of peace feels so abstract right now; he craves it, but he can't imagine actually feeling it, not fully. In a conflicted way he envies his twenty-one-year-old self who didn't give a shit what he did or who he hurt. His youthful arrogance and selfish desires overrode his conscience time and time again.

He sighs and rubs his hands over his sallow face, pinches the hollow contours of his cheeks between his fingers, trying to wake himself up a bit. He really needs to get going.

A waiter appears at his table offering a coffee top-up and Fenix glances up at him. 'I'm all done, thanks, mate,' he says to the young, ginger-haired lad, then recognises him as Marla's son from the B&B. Rye, if he remembers correctly.

'Right you are,' says Rye, taking his empty mug away.

As Fenix shrugs on his coat, he watches Rye interact with who he presumes is the café owner, a middle-aged woman wearing a red apron and a friendly smile. They seem to make a good team, and he admires the lad's work ethic – helping his mum out at the B&B as well as working here. Fenix used to hate the frequent cleaning work his dad forced him and his brother to do once old Mrs Roberts next door had popped her clogs. The state some people left caravans in used to astound him. And the smells in the summer were rank – stifling heat blended with sweat and stained bedsheets and blocked up toilets. At first they only did a half-arsed job, chucking rubbish and dirty crockery in cupboards and under the hastily made beds before sneaking off to the dunes to smoke spliffs. They didn't get away with it for long though. Their dad was always waiting for them with a face like thunder and would give them clips round their earholes as well as an earful about what lazy little wastes of spaces they were if the caravans weren't cleaned to his high standards. If they dared to answer back, he'd force them to their knees and make them lick the underside of a toilet seat. Later, they'd pretend to laugh about it between themselves but the insults and the humiliation and the fierce, flat palms to their heads really stung.

He goes to the counter to pay for his coffee and as he taps his card against the contactless machine, the café owner glances between him and Rye.

'Any relation?' she asks, pointing at the lad.

Fenix is confused. 'Sorry?' he says, his brows scrunching.

She nudges Rye and he stops buttering a teacake and turns around.

'Long-lost family member?' she asks, signalling at Fenix and chuckling, her crow's feet crinkling. 'The resemblance is there, to my eye anyway!'

'Is it?' Fenix is taken aback at the suggestion and Rye shrugs then shakes his head, just as perplexed. They both laugh, united in awkwardness.

'No?' says the woman. 'Ignore me then. Must be one of those coincidences!' She looks beyond Fenix and smiles at another customer approaching the counter. 'Yes, love, what can I get you?' she asks them. Fenix shoots a glance at Rye. The lad seems frozen, lost in thought, holding the butter knife limply. After a second, he blinks, comes to back to life and resumes his task.

Pulling on his beanie hat, Fenix leaves the café. The woman's words are needling at him, creating a strange sensation within him, even stranger than chemo dripping into his veins. He looks back, watching Rye through the window, studying the lad's movements and mannerisms as best he can from here, the prickling feeling growing sharper, stronger. No. He shuts the thought down. It's impossible, isn't it? He thinks back to his reckless youth, all his dalliances, all his liaisons. No, he tells himself again. He's been through this in therapy – using light-hearted, respectable-sounding words rather than naming his actions exactly what they were: rape.

Could one of those rapes have resulted in a son?

3RD MARCH 1997
SCARLET

Our new GCSE tutor started today. What a joke. It's literally weeks until our exams and we've got to get used to someone new thanks to Rubie being her usual nasty bitch self and driving the other one away by being as difficult and disruptive as she could. It's like she doesn't want any of us to succeed. Not that I liked the other tutor either. It was pretty obvious she thought Rosalie was cleverer than me and Rubie. I mean, it's true, Rosie is the smartest one of us, but it's not nice to be reminded every session and talked down to like that. We can't help that we've missed so much school since Mum got worse.

Rosie is Mum's favourite too. She always has been, which makes me sad. Mum always says she loves us all the same, but it must be hard for her to split her heart into three. She doesn't always act like she loves us equally because she's always stroking Rosie's hair and telling her how proud she is of her. It makes Rubie so angry and jealous too, so she sometimes locks Rosalie in her room so she can have Mum all to herself for a while. Rosie doesn't even bang on the door and shout to be let out anymore in case it upsets Mum. She just accepts it now. Or maybe she's glad to be on her own for a bit and away from Rubie.

I wish I could be on my own sometimes too. Rubie thinks she rules everything, including me, and I hate it! I can't wait until I'm old enough to leave stupid old Stonethorpe-On-Sea. Rubie forced me to make a pact with her that we'll leave together on our eighteenth birthday and move to a big city and get modelling jobs, but I've decided I'm getting a flat of my own instead. I'm sick of having those two for sisters!

MONDAY 30TH OCTOBER 2017

CHAPTER TWENTY-ONE

ALLIE

I sit cross-legged on my bed at the B&B, my laptop open in front of me and Mason's articles spread out next to me. I've read them all carefully as well as made additional notes on the conversations I've had with the locals over the past few days. I'm all ready for Ralph's call, which Ebony has informed me, via text message, is scheduled for noon. He rings right on time.

'Hit me with the updates,' he says as soon as I answer, dispensing with unnecessary greetings as usual.

'So, I've spoken to Marla Ryerson the B&B owner, Maeve Hodgeson at the post office, Caroline and Phillip Roberts who own the site the fair used to pitch on, and of course Mason McKenzie the ex-journalist,' I report.

'What have you got – anything juicy?' he asks.

I inwardly cringe at his inappropriate use of the word "juicy" in relation to an unsolved crime but choose not to remark on it; due to the amount of information I need to impart, this phone call is likely to be longer than my preferred five minute maximum. Referring to my notes, I briefly outline each conversation and interview in turn, obviously sticking only to the relevant facts and omitting the fact that I spent the night screwing the ex-journalist's brains out. Ralph hums thoughtfully on the other end of the phone as I divulge what I've been told and the hums progress to excited gasps as I reveal people's theories, including Mason's about Silas being the culprit for the Sanderson attack. Finally, I have to admit that the more I found out, the more the different versions of the stories didn't seem to add up and that most opinions seemed to be rooted in biases. I conclude by telling him that neither the police nor Mason could find any definitive evidence of who did what, so the cold case remains unsolved.

'Still, that's a lot to be getting on with – well done you!' he exclaims. 'Do you think you've got enough material to start drafting the book now?'

'I think I can definitely shape the outline and make a start on drafting the first couple of chapters. It'd mean staying another night though, just to double-check anything I need to first hand.' The words are out of my mouth before I'm even aware I'm saying it.

'Okay, I think we can stretch the budget to one more night, if that's what you need to hit the ground running with this. As long as you've got the outline and the first few chapters ready for the meeting in London on Friday, that's good enough for me,' he says.

'Thanks, Ralph. I appreciate it,' I say, not surprised he has agreed so easily. I've googled the overnight rate for the B&B and it's a pittance. I've more than earned my comped stay here so far. My gaze drifts to the photo I've re-stuck to the dressing table mirror. The photo I take with me everywhere of a young girl cradling a newborn baby, her traumatised expression frozen in time. She looks older than her years, shell-shocked at becoming a mother, but there's also a strength in her eyes and in the protective way she holds the child.

'No problem,' he says. 'You've done good work, Allie.

Remember to utilise Ebony for any image-gathering or historical fact-checking or whatnot. Just email her a list. She'll extend your booking until tomorrow too.'

He hangs up before I can respond as my attention is now elsewhere anyway.

Leaving my phone on the bed, I rise and walk over to the photo, plucking it from the mirror to examine it more closely. The girl's face is so familiar yet so alien at the same time. 'It wasn't your fault,' I whisper to her, as I've told her many times before. She doesn't answer me. She never has. But I hope she truly believes me. I press the photo back onto the glass and reach higher to touch the delicate gold locket hanging from the corner of the mirror, rubbing my thumb gently across its shiny surface and the rose motif engraved in the centre. I stare at the photo for a long time, my mind meandering to familiar but miserable places, my heart as unsettled as the choppy sea outside.

My phone rings, puncturing my maudlin reverie. I smile when I see Mason's name on my screen as a respectable, non-needy amount of time has now passed since we last saw each other.

'Hey. How's your day going?' he asks when I answer.

'Not bad,' I reply, sitting back on the bed.

'I've been thinking about what you said about Phillip Roberts being shady,' he says. I'm pleasantly surprised that he's leading with this rather than our antics last night. 'I must admit, he flew right under my radar, and his father. I never considered them plausible suspects. I'm wondering now if I should have.' He sounds frustrated and I understand why. This case defined his whole career and for new information to come to light twenty years later, however tenuous, must be exasperating.

'But they were questioned by the police at the time too, weren't they?'

'Yes. All the local men were. And neither of the Roberts had a criminal record then.' He pauses. 'Nor since.'

I smile, knowing that means he's checked. 'Friends on the force?' I ask.

'Once a journalist always a journalist.' He laughs softly.

'Doesn't mean they're not guilty though,' I say.

'Listen to you. For all your protests about being *just* a ghostwriter, you're actually interested in this case. And you've managed to raise a few interesting questions while conducting your interviews. We could have done with you back then to help solve the mystery.'

'What about you?' I ask.

'What about me what?'

'Well, you know everything about the Sanderson case inside out,' I say, my pulse quickening, unsure of his reaction. 'You've researched it, pored over it, written scores of articles about it. It's the perfect cover.'

The silence on the line stretches between us, my heart pounding as I wait for his response, wondering if this is an act of self-sabotage or something I've dragged from my subconscious and daring to voice.

'That's quite the supposition, Allie,' he says finally. There's an edge to his voice that makes me think I might have touched a nerve.

I force a laugh. 'Can you blame me for thinking it? You know more about the attacks than anyone.'

'Are you suggesting I committed the Sanderson attack in '97 or the one in '98? Or both?'

'Maybe you committed the first crime and then a copycat committed the second?' I say flippantly.

'So now I inspired a copycat attacker?' he says, sounding more amused now. 'Wow. I'm dangerous. Or maybe I was just doing my job well and reporting the facts as I discovered them.'

'Maybe,' I concede, smirking into the phone, glad he hasn't taken offence to my questions. I won't ever filter what I want to say to anyone I'm involved with but him not being a dick about it is pleasing. Claudia was often dickish about my bold statements, especially if they referred to her precious Shelley.

'Well, if you're not sure you're welcome to come over again later and interrogate me for as long as you like. I'll even provide food to sustain you, in case it turns into an all-nighter.'

I like his flirty tone and I'm tempted by his offer, especially as I've apparently decided to stay another night in this weird little town. I check the time. I need to get this work done but I do also need to eat. And there's something about Mason that really draws me in.

'How about providing a birthday cake?' I ask.

'It's your birthday?'

'Tomorrow. Halloween,' I confirm.

'Same as the Sanderson sisters,' he says, without missing a beat.

'I know. Freaky coincidence, right?'

'Well, I think I can stretch to a cake, and maybe even candles, but only if you'll still be here at midnight to make a wish on your actual birthday.'

'Deal.' I smile at the thought of it. 'I'll see you tonight.'

'Looking forward to it, Allie,' he says.

We say goodbye and I hang up the phone. I cross to the window, needing to expel some nervous energy. A mist has descended outside, and the scene is slightly opaque, like a veil has been drawn over Stonethorpe. My gaze is drawn once again to the photo stuck to my mirror and the locket hung above it and I think about the birthday wish that Mason has promised me at midnight. There's only one thing I ever wish for even though it's an impossibility: to be able to erase the most hideously traumatic event of my life, or at least find some sort of meaning to it or revenge for it. As it's twenty years too late to turn back time, it can never be erased, so I guess I'll be blowing out my candles and focusing on the second option this birthday.

TUESDAY 31ST OCTOBER 2017

CHAPTER TWENTY-TWO

ALLIE

The ping of a text wakes me, and I groan as I roll over, sleep still clinging to me like a sloth. I must have forgotten to turn my phone to do not disturb when I got back to the B&B last night – or rather the early hours of this morning – and I still haven't had enough shut-eye yet. Fragments of consciousness stream in and snapshots of my night with Mason remind me why I feel so exhausted now. Exhausted but sated after a heady combination of good wine and hot sex. The memory simmers before more recollections slowly start to drip in: it's my last day in Stonethorpe-On-Sea and it's Halloween – my birthday.

I reach for my phone and squint against the screen's glare. I'm surprised to see the message is from Claudia. My heart jolts. I open it, anticipating another snippy break-up admin text, something that will inevitably ruin my sleep-deprived but relatively good mood. Instead, it simply reads:

Happy birthday.

That's it. Two words. No kiss. No exclamation mark. No cute GIF or emoji to soften the starkness. She may as well not have bothered. I stare at the message, winded, the disappointment gut-punching much harder than expected. I shouldn't care. We've broken up. I've spent the last two nights with Mason feeling desired and appreciated, which is more than she made me feel towards the end of our relationship. I don't need her to make a special effort for me. I wouldn't even want to revive our dead-in-the-water relationship, even if she begged me to, which she never would. But I can't help my mind drifting back to when we first met and how besotted we were with each other in the beginning. I'd even allowed myself to imagine us as older women, fulfilled and sophisticated and serene, holidaying on luxury cruise ships, thousands of miles away from her awful sister. Or better yet, inviting Shelley along and anonymously engineering an additional trip overboard for her; a truly tragic turn of events. But Claudia and I weren't to be once the hairline cracks widened to uncrossable chasms.

I delete the message from my phone. The words disappear but it'll be a long time before I can delete thoughts of Claudia so easily, especially as I'm heading back to Leeds later today. As sad as it'll be to return to an empty apartment, I'm excited to see my gorgeous little Story. Cat cuddles always cheer me up.

A soft knock at the door makes me jump. My pulse quickens as I remember my mysterious non-visitor from yesterday. This time, however, there's no mistaking who it is as Marla's voice soon follows the knock.

'Coo-ee, Allie, love. It's only me.'

I turn on the lamp, slip out of bed and pull an oversized hoodie over my long T-shirt, pulling the hood up to cover my naked, dishevelled hair.

The landlady is standing on the landing with a tray bearing a steaming cup of tea and a saucer of biscuits.

'Happy birthday,' she says, beaming.

I blink, startled. 'How did you know it was my birthday?' I ask, sharper than intended.

Her smile falters at my slightly frosty tone and she looks a bit put out.

'We always ask for guests' dates of birth when they book in,' she explains, a touch defensive. 'I remembered yours as it was Halloween. Not that we acknowledge that in Stonethorpe, for obvious reasons,' she adds in a stage whisper, proffering the tray. I take it, softening, remembering that Ebony had filled out the booking form.

'Thanks very much, Marla,' I say, placing the tray on the dressing table beneath my photo and necklace.

She waves my gratitude away. 'Oh, it's nothing much, just a cuppa and some biccies seeing as you didn't come down for breakfast, but I hope you enjoy them, dear. And if you need anything else, you just let me know.'

'You've looked after me really well already, what with the cooked breakfasts and the clean towels just appearing here in my room.'

'The fresh towels are my Rye's doing. He's a good little housekeeper, isn't he? In and out like a thief in the night – not that he would ever steal from guests, mind, but you know what I mean.' She chuckles at her own joke, her pride in her son evident. 'Anyway, I'll let you get on. Many happy returns,' she says, giving a brief wave as she turns and heads back downstairs.

I close the door behind her and move to the dressing table. I take a sip of tea and a bite of a biscuit and feel strangely emotional about this kind gesture from a relative stranger who has made a bigger fuss for my birthday than Claudia. I glance at my reflection in the mirror. My pale face looks almost translucent in the lamplight, even with the remains of yesterday's make-up still clinging to my skin and eyelashes. My gaze moves to the gold locket hanging on the corner of the mirror, and then to the photograph stuck to the glass. I think about what I need to do before I leave this town. About who I want to be.

I set my tea down and lug my wheelie case up onto the bed. Unzipping it, I pull out the third wig I brought with me, just in case. The black one. The one I always wear on my birthday, the one that makes me look like I did when I was younger, like the girl I used to be. The girl who ceased to exist twenty years ago. I must have known deep down that I was going to stay until today all along.

Taking my hoodie off, I slip the wig on, adjusting it carefully until it sits just right. I stare at myself in the mirror and my transformation is immediate. The long black strands fall around my pale face, not only transforming how I look but how I feel too. Next, I tenderly unhook the gold locket and fasten the chain around my neck. The girl staring back at me isn't the woman I am now, but someone else, full of inner scars, sadness and secrets. Just like the girl in the photo. I inhale sharply as a thought strikes me – Marla said Rye was responsible for putting clean towels in the rooms. He must have been the one who moved my picture. If it was him, why?

CHAPTER TWENTY-THREE

FENIX

Fenix stands at the Sandersons' door clutching a bouquet of red roses. His hand trembles slightly because he's been holding the flowers for a few minutes, trying to pluck up the courage to knock. He's frightened of Silas appearing and roaring at him again, he's frightened of seeing Rosalie and facing his shameful past, but he's also frightened of not seeing Rosalie and never getting to say what he so desperately needs to say to her, face to face. His breaths are shallow, and his heart is hammering in his chest at the thought of this whole trip being a futile waste of time. And time is now the one thing he can't afford to waste.

The old farmhouse seems to loom before him, just like the last time he came, large and ominous yet practically decrepit. But today there are no signs of life, no shadow at the upstairs window, no sounds from within, no lumbering drunk ordering him off the property. The memory of Silas's rage is still fresh in his mind, his declaration that Rosalie is dead to the Sanderson family echoing in his ears. Fenix doesn't know what to believe but he knows this is his best lead. He has to try again.

He takes a deep breath and finally knocks on the heavy wooden door, forcing himself to stand still, to face whatever's coming head-on. The fear of going to his grave without seeing this through is greater than his fear of Silas right now and he feels light-headed at the possibility of fulfilling this promise to himself, of actually speaking to Rosalie. If she really has been here all this time, existing as a ghost, hidden away from the world because of what he did to her, he's willing to do or say whatever it takes to help her heal. And that in turn will lessen his guilt and salve his soul.

The sound of dogs barking makes him jump, sending his heart rate soaring even more. He can hear their claws tapping and scratching on the other side of the door, clearly frustrated at not being able to break through to him. He steels himself, clutches the bouquet even tighter, and licks his dry lips. He's ready. But despite the dogs' reaction, the door remains closed. His knock remains unanswered. After a couple more minutes, he steps back onto the gravel driveway and scrutinises the frontage of the house, but it all remains shut and still. Disappointment fills all the hollow parts of him, generating an intense sour feeling much worse than he was expecting. He hangs his head and huffs out a heavy sigh. He'd geared himself up so much and now what? Shaking his head, he carefully places the bouquet on the porch step and starts to walk away, heading to the church as planned. And then he has an idea. He doubles back on himself and retrieves a pen from his bag and the serviette he absent-mindedly picked up from the café from his pocket and writes a note. When he's done, he tucks it beneath the flowers.

Feeling lighter already, and with one last remnant of hope in his heart, he turns and walks away.

The lightness has all but disappeared by the time Fenix arrives at the entrance to the graveyard surrounding the church. It has started to drizzle and the autumn leaves carpeting the path have become slick and shiny. The sky itself is slate grey, as it has been this whole visit, mirroring his now morose mood and making the town seem even more desolate than usual. His prickly thoughts plague him – memories of his youth, shameful scenes of his sins and distressing fears about his future. His head feels like it's going to explode and sometimes he wants to crack it open himself, to release all the guilt and worry like pus from an infected abscess.

He waits on a bench near the gate, brooding for a short while, and then opts to do a slow circuit of the grounds. He feels better when he's moving – it reminds him that he still has some control over his ailing body. As he rounds the corner of the church tower, he catches sight of a woman entering the graveyard. His heart stutters and his breath catches in his throat as he stops and watches her pick her way between the graves. She's wearing a coat with a hood but the way she walks, the way she moves, reinforces the recognition.

It's her, he's sure of it. She found the flowers and the note, and she came to meet him. It's Rosalie.

CHAPTER TWENTY-FOUR

ALLIE

Zipping my coat up to my chin, I follow the arc of the low drystone church walls before turning through the gap onto the main path running through the graveyard. I pull my hood up to protect my wig from the drizzle as well as disguise my appearance, although the grounds are completely deserted, which pleases me. I want to be on my own with the dead today. After taking a few steps I veer off onto the grass, wending my way through the few skeletal trees and weathered gravestones until I finally find the one I'm looking for. I stop in front of it, tears already blurring my vision. It's a simple headstone bearing only a name and two dates. It's too plain for someone who meant so much. I crouch down to gently trace the inscription.

'Hello, Mum,' I whisper, my voice full of emotion. 'It's me.'

Even those few words catch in my throat and become sobs. Soon I'm consumed by them, my body shaking with them, the seal I've kept screwed so tightly for so many years now broken. I fall to my knees and allow my tears to flow freely yet soon struggle to breathe as great gulping gasps overwhelm me. Back then I never imagined that the next time I saw my mother would be like this. This wasn't how things were supposed to turn out.

After a while I manage to calm myself, or perhaps I've just worn myself out. My sobs subside into soft hiccups, my breaths still shallow. Despite the drizzle, I stay kneeling before the headstone, not wanting to leave, not wanting to sever mine and Mum's connection now we've been reunited. I close my eyes and imagine she's sitting there with me. She's just as she was before everything bad happened. In my head I talk to her, tell her I love her, tell her I'm sorry for not coming sooner. The words pour out of me like a confession, unfiltered and unrestrained. I tell her all about my life, my job, my relationships. About my regrets, my achievements, my insecurities. I tell her about Claudia and Story. I tell her about Mason. I tell her about the girl in the photo and what being back here means to me. I tell her everything until there's nothing left to say.

Eventually, I stand, brush the dirt from my hands and knees, and take one last look at the gravestone. 'I'll come back again one day, Mum,' I promise her. I twirl then tuck a few loose long black strands of hair back inside my hood, even though I already doubt I'll ever wear this wig again now. I'm not who I was anymore.

As I tread the cracked stone path on my way back to the car, something catches the corner of my eye, and I whip my head towards the far side of the church, certain I saw someone dart past. It must have been the vicar that Mason told me about, one of his suggested interviewees that I haven't followed up with. Well, it's too late now and Ralph seems more than happy with what I've got so far. I might ask Ebony to contact him, send him a few questions on my behalf if I need a bit more padding for the book. Plus, I feel completely wrung out after visiting Mum and I definitely don't want to meet the latest Stonethorpe vicar looking like I currently do, like a ghoulish replica of its most infamous residents. It may be Halloween, but

I just want to get back to the B&B, get this costume off, and drive back to Leeds.

I'm almost at the car when I get that strange sensation again, like someone is watching me. The feeling is unmistakeable, and goosebumps rise on my skin as I scan the grounds. But there's nobody around. I quicken my step, pressing the fob to open the car door, and that's when I hear it. A male voice calling a name that I haven't heard in twenty years.

My name: Rosalie.

21ST JUNE 1997
SCARLET

Today was actually pretty good for once. Mum treated us for finishing our exams, so me and Rubie decided to go and see Liar Liar at the cinema. It was hilarious! Rubie laughed so hard at one point she nearly choked on her popcorn – I wish! That would have been the funniest thing of all! It was nice to feel like we were "normal" sisters, even if it was just for a couple of hours. It was easy to pretend when we were sitting in the dark and not speaking to each other! Rosalie didn't want to come with us (as usual), so she stayed at home (as usual), probably sucking up to Mum or reading one of her precious books. She always acts like she's better than us!

Anyway, that's not the big news of the day... the big news is that we walked past Sandy Crest Caravan Park on the way to the cinema and saw the new family that have moved in and taken over. They have two sons and OMG... talk about gorgeous! Especially the tall one with the dark-red hair and the earring and strong, muscly arms! Seriously, he looks like he belongs in Take That! Of course, Rubie bagsied him before I could even say I fancied him, just like she used to take my Ken dolls without asking. Now I won't be able to even ogle him without her having a go that I'm lusting after her "future boyfriend". She's such a cow and wants every boy for herself! But she can't control what I think about so I'm going to fantasise about him whenever I want!

I bet all the girls in town will fancy him too, but you never know, he might actually notice me one day. Not Rubie, but ME! Mum said when Mrs Roberts rang the other day, she told her the new family's surname is Clifton. I've already practised what my signature would be if I got married to the brother I like best when I'm older. Mrs Scarlet Clifton... how good does that sound!

CHAPTER TWENTY-FIVE

RUBIE

After checking that Scarlet is sleeping upstairs, Rubie sits at her desk in the farmhouse's front sitting room. She reads the note left for Rosalie for about the fiftieth time, tracing her finger over the phone number written under the name *Fenix*.

I came back to tell you I'm sorry. Please forgive me.

She wants to call it, but she doesn't own a mobile phone and Silas still checks the landline itemised bills. Instead, she types it into Google. Nothing but two random websites come back. She adds *Fenix* and hits enter again. This time she gets the answer that her search did not match any documents. Not being tech savvy enough to know what else she could try, Rubie sighs in defeat, knowing it was a long shot anyway.

Her fingers hover back over the keyboard, hesitating for only a couple of seconds before typing in the same search she's done hundreds of times before: *Sanderson sisters attack 1997*. The familiar hits appear on the screen, most linking to newspaper articles by a journalist named Mason McKenzie. In a warped way it used to thrill her, seeing her name in print, hoping the coverage would lead to a break in their case, but it never did. Now she and Scarlet are old news, and the articles are just regurgitated tales, no better than historical fiction.

Still, she clicks on one of the articles from early 1998 and begins to read even though she's practically memorised everything written about them back then. The haunting details about the attack, the same unanswered questions, the references to possible suspects that nothing ever came of. The familiar sickening feeling in her stomach returns as she scrolls through the texts. And then, in one, the mention of Rosalie's disappearance on New Year's Eve, just a couple of weeks before Rubie and Scarlet were finally discharged from the hospital. Rubie always hated her for that, for not even bothering to say goodbye. The way she callously abandoned them, simultaneously sending their mother's already precarious health further downhill. And then she stubbornly stayed away with whoever she chose to shack up with, subjecting them to Silas and his savage ways, leaving Rubie to shakily hold the shattered pieces of the Sanderson family together. But how could she, when it was already broken beyond repair?

Or maybe Rosalie didn't choose to leave. Perhaps whoever attacked Rubie and Scarlet wanted Rosalie too, and bided their time to take her, or kill her. But Rubie's gut has always told her that was less likely. She really feels that her sister is still out there somewhere, and that belief has been reinforced now a strange man is looking for her.

She shoves the keyboard forward, rests her arms on the desk and lets her head fall onto them. A tornado of emotions swirls within her, dragging an assortment of scenarios into its inescapable funnel: a glamorous Rosalie living in a London townhouse, a sun-kissed Rosalie sipping wine in a rustic château, and the worst one of all, the one that tortures her the most, a contented Rosalie surrounded by her children and husband in a beautiful home in the countryside, with dogs and horses and a meadow full of flowers. Wherever Rosalie is, she's free of the rusty old chains that keep Rubie tethered here and she can't bear the longing, the jealousy, the not knowing for even one more day, especially today – their birthday.

She makes a decision. She decides she's going to be brave and go into town and ask around to find out if the stranger is still here, and who he might be. She's going to find him and hopefully finally solve at least part of the mystery about her missing sister.

Rubie stands and crosses to the door, passing the old chest of drawers tucked into the recessed alcove. She stops abruptly, remembering the letter. The one Rosalie apparently sent their mum a few months after she disappeared. Uncle Silas had read it aloud to them when it arrived, and Rubie is sure he squirrelled it away in here with her mum's death certificate and other important paperwork. She yanks open the top drawer but it's just full of bits and bobs, so she tries the second drawer. This one's full of loose documents, mainly old utility bills and scribbled notes on the back of torn, empty envelopes. Kneeling, she tries the third and final drawer and discovers two old photo albums and a large hexagonal biscuit tin, which she recognises as the tin her mum used to keep her sewing kit in. Rubie chokes back tears as a wave of loss and nostalgia overcomes her. She touches the lid, tracing the raised lettering and decorative border around the edges, picturing her mum sitting in her floral armchair lovingly mending one of Scarlet's soft toys with a needle and thread. Scarlet was always the roughest with all their things when they were younger; she hated to share, especially her Barbie and Ken dolls.

Rubie lifts the tin out of the drawer and places it on her lap and as she does, she spies an old but familiar notebook that was nestled underneath. Her pulse quickens and her eyes widen.

She can't believe it: it's Scarlet's old diary from when they were teenagers. Many a time Rubie had found her writing in it ferociously with a secretive, childlike intensity. It was the one thing Scarlet would never let her touch let alone read, and try as she might, Rubie was never able to sniff it out because Scarlet changed where she hid it so often. It drove her crazy and often made her question their bond because if she couldn't work out her sister's hiding places then how close were they really?

And now she's found it when she wasn't even looking for it! She grabs it and holds it in her hands with a prickling sixth sense that it may contain more than secrets. It may contain a key to the past. Setting aside thoughts of Rosalie for the moment, the urge to snoop too strong, she flips open the cover of the diary.

The handwriting on the first half of the first page is neat – Scarlet starts by dotting every i with a flower – but it quickly descends into messy, scattered scrawls. Rubie squints, struggling to decipher it initially but as she gets used to it, the wriggly words eventually become clearer, as does the sound of Scarlet's voice through them. Most of the entries seem feverish and full of exclamation marks, but as she impatiently flicks through the pages, Rubie spots two particular initials that catch her interest: FC. She knows instinctively that they stand for Felton Clifton. She reads rapidly, turning page after page, discovering that like her, Scarlet also had feelings for the older boy, fantasised about being his girlfriend, but kept it to herself because she knew how much Rubie wanted him. Yet she hated Rubie for it.

Scarlet lays it all out in her diary. Her language is coarse, and her ire is blatant and transparent. Rubie is shocked by the ferocity of her outpourings, this hidden, toxic side of her sister, but she can't stop reading. Her breath catches in her throat and her hands tremble as she delves deeper into Scarlet's psyche. The diary is almost full and as Rubie nears the end of the populated pages, she stops on an entry from a few days before their attack.

> 23rd October 1997
>
> *Well, well, well... Seems I have more than one absolute bitch of a sister. Ravishing Rubie has competition for FC's affection, and I don't mean me. Guess who I saw getting hot and heavy in the barn? Only sweet little mouse Saint Rosalie. Her and FC were lying on the dirty, hay-covered floor like animals in heat – gross! She was letting him rut her from behind and her hair was all loose and fanned out like she thought she was a movie star or something.*
>
> *The best part about it is that all this time Rubie was paranoid about me swooping in and stealing FC from under her nose (which I definitely could do if I wanted to!) when Rosalie was the real threat all along. Rubie's going to lose her mind when she finds out. Her head will actually explode and her basic brain will splat all over the place. I wanted to run inside and tell her straight away so I could see her face scrunch up like a rat's, which it does when she's really angry or upset, but I think it'll be more fun to keep it a secret for now. It's going to be so hilarious watching her get ready for Kayleigh's party on Sunday, plastering her face with her new make-up and putting on her sexy new clothes, knowing she's going to throw herself at FC like an unpaid prostitute. But the whole time I'll know that if she gets him, she'll be nothing but sloppy seconds. Ha ha ha!*

Rubie clamps a hand over her mouth. She's reeling, her stomach churning with disgust and disbelief even though the hard evidence is right there in front of her. Both of her own sisters hated her enough to go behind her back and screw her over – one quite literally.

With a sudden, burning fury, Rubie stands up and storms out of the room, straight to the front door. She yanks it open, pulls her arm back and in a dramatic fit of pique, hurls Scarlet's diary as far as she can. She pants, clenches her fists at her sides, and then she's startled by the sight of the bouquet on the porch step. Red roses. When did they appear? She stares at the flowers for a few moments, feeling like she's hallucinating. Then a flicker of joy blooms within her as she wonders if the beautiful bouquet is for her, a surprise birthday gift from someone who still remembers. She snatches the roses up and as she does, she notices a square of paper beneath it. Picking it up, she sees it's a serviette, another note.

> *Rosalie,*
> *Please meet me at the church today and allow me the chance to explain.*
> *F x*

It's the same handwriting that was on the card from Fenix. She frowns, considering that letter F and the kiss. She remembers the initials in Scarlet's diary. She thinks about what Scarlet wrote, about what she saw Rosalie doing in the barn. Could it be... could Fenix be Felton Clifton?

CHAPTER TWENTY-SIX

FENIX

Rosalie doesn't react to Fenix calling her name straight away and for a few seconds he thinks he must have been mistaken, got carried away in the moment, drunk on premature relief and gratitude that she actually came. But then she slowly turns to face him and he's able to get a proper look at her. He was sure she was Rosalie, but something seems off now.

Maybe it's just that they're so much older – after all, he's a shadow of the strapping young man he once was. Her face looks so different, but it seems like she's got the same black hair she had back then, even though he can only see a few wet strands, and there's something recognisable about her eyes. She looks a bit like the woman he saw leaving the bungalow next to the old fair site on Sunday – that writer, except she had pink hair. He shakes his head; a lot of weird stuff and coincidences have been happening in this town. Regardless, he knows in his soul this is Rosalie. He feels a connection to her, even from here, even after what happened between them.

She still hasn't spoken and he's scrambling for what to say or do next. The rain is coming down heavier now and he desperately wants to step closer to her, to confirm that she got his peace-offering bouquet, but he keeps his distance, not wanting to appear intimidating or overbearing. He's been rehearsing this moment for years, playing out every possible scenario, but he hasn't accounted for her silence. Maybe it's her who's mute, not Scarlet. Now he's here, now he needs to actually say the words aloud, they escape him. He takes a deep breath, forcing himself to just go for it, feel his way as he goes, bend whichever way she dictates, but before he's able to utter anything, she speaks first.

'Felton Clifton.'

Hearing his old name again, the one he's worked so hard to leave behind, sends a shock through him. No one's called him that for years, not even his wife. Not since he legally changed it to Fenix, burning his old life to ashes and rising again as a reformed man. Hearing it now, from her lips, feels toxic.

The hatred emanates from her, and he swallows, his mouth dry.

'You remember me,' he says, stating the obvious.

'I remember you.' Her lip curls in disgust and she fixes him with a look so loaded with contempt that his legs feel unsteady. He feels a tightness in his chest, twin fists of disgrace and remorse squeezing him from within.

'I wanted...' he begins but he doesn't know how to continue the sentence despite the mini pep talk he's just given himself. He shrugs helplessly.

'You wanted,' she agrees with him, nodding but not breaking eye contact. 'You wanted and you took what you wanted.' Her voice is as hard as the concrete and granite headstones around them, and she's only just begun.

Fenix shifts, uncomfortable in his own skin, and in this necessary interaction. Necessary but now even more excruciating than he imagined.

'I'm sorry,' he says at last. 'I'm truly sorry for what I did to you.' His voice cracks but he carries on, gathering momentum now. 'I was young and stupid and reckless and no, I'm sorry, that sounds like I'm making excuses and I'm not. I want to face what I did, take responsibility at last. What I did was unforgivable, and I know I hurt you.' He pauses, takes a deep shuddering breath. 'I hate who I was back then, but I didn't hate you. I loved you. I'm so sorry, Rosalie.'

'Allie,' she says, coldly.

He shakes his head, confused. 'Sorry?'

'I stopped being Rosalie a long time ago. My name is Allie now. And the only reason I'm telling you that is so that you understand how meaningless your apology is. You can't apologise to someone who doesn't even exist and, more importantly, someone who doesn't even exist cannot grant you forgiveness. So, it looks like you'll be burning in hell forever.'

She spits out the words so articulately, eyes blazing, fists clenched. He's seen this before plenty of times in therapy sessions he's conducted or supervised, when victims are given the opportunity to read impact statements to whoever has wronged them. After all, they are what prompted him to want to find Rosalie in the first place. But he never envisioned he'd feel this wretched, didn't think he could plummet to even further depths of revulsion for his past actions.

Fenix drops his gaze, unable to bear the weight of her disdain any longer. 'Well, you'll get your wish because I'm dying,' he says, in a last-ditch attempt to turn the conversation around. He would have preferred not to admit this for fear of being accused of emotional manipulation, but he can't leave yet, not without at least trying one last thing to make her see how sincere he is. 'I've got cancer. It's... it's terminal.'

To his surprise, she laughs. A short, sharp bark that morphs into a hearty chuckle. After a minute she stops abruptly and resumes her scornful expression. 'Couldn't have happened to a nicer guy.'

The insult was obvious yet it's still unexpected and it takes his breath away. The silence hangs between them, heavy and awkward, and they are both now sodden to the skin. Yet neither of them moves, trapped in this bizarre stalemate. Fenix feels as though he's unravelling, like he could just collapse and spool onto the path, mingle with the rain and the leaves until he disintegrates away to nothing. Maybe that's all he deserves – to cease existing, just like that.

And yet he thinks of the time they spent together in the dunes behind the fair site. Of the trust they built, the closeness they cultivated, the sweet kisses she bestowed on him willingly, consensually, back in 1997. Surely that all counts for something? Suddenly a fuse lights within him and he's angry. Angry that she won't accept his heartfelt apology, that she's making him feel even worse than he already does, that she won't believe the honest words of a dying man.

It's time for a change of tack.

CHAPTER TWENTY-SEVEN

RUBIE

Rubie doesn't know what to do first. She's overwhelmed with emotion, frustration, information, all of it. She's learned more in the past half an hour than she's known for the past two decades, and now, because of this note, there's a chance she might find out even more – today. Her birthday. Scarlet's birthday. Rosalie's birthday. Of course, this is what the flowers are for. Felton's gift to her whore of a sister. And what exactly does he need to explain, to apologise for? All Rubie knows is that she wants to hear it too. And while he's at it, perhaps he can explain to her why she wasn't good enough to be his girlfriend, but her own sister was.

But before she can do that, before she can even leave the house, she needs to speak to Scarlet and then secure her.

Rubie thunders up the stairs and flings open the bedroom door. Oak and Elm immediately jump up to greet her, but she herds them away and stomps over to the bed where Scarlet lies. Her eyes are open, and her body is still as she just stares at the ceiling. Normally Rubie would soften at this sight, feel sympathy for her poor, locked-in, silent sister, but not today, not now she knows what a double-crossing little bitch she was. And maybe still is.

She leans down close to Scarlet's face and waits for her eyes to lock on to hers. Rubie smiles widely.

'Thank you for the birthday present,' she says sweetly.

Scarlet pinches her eyebrows together questioningly.

'The gift of insight,' Rubie says. 'Very thoughtful. Or should I say thought-provoking?'

Scarlet blinks.

Rubie drops the smile and replaces it with a hard glare.

'I found your diary from 1997,' she clarifies. 'Quite the novel.' She pauses, watching Scarlet carefully for a reaction but her sister simply gazes at her. Rubie is trembling; she's had enough.

'You never told me!' she shouts, her voice shaking with rage. 'You never told me you saw Felton and Rosalie in the barn! You knew I was in love with him... You let me make a fool of myself with him at the party! You wanted me to!'

Scarlet flinches at the force of Rubie's wrath and then her face crumples, tears welling in her eyes. But it won't wash with Rubie this time. She has more questions, needs more answers.

'What other secrets have you been keeping all these years? What else do you know?' She grabs Scarlet's notebook and pencil from the windowsill and throws them onto the bed. 'Write it down! Tell me!'

Scarlet covers her face with her hands and turns over, burrowing further under the duvet.

'Tell me!' screams Rubie, pummelling the mound Scarlet has created in the bed.

The dogs begin to whine and bark, picking up on Rubie's distress, and she realises interrogating her sister is utterly futile. Scarlet hasn't spoken in twenty years; she's not going to start today. And even if she did, Rubie wouldn't believe a word that came out of her lying little mouth. No, if she wants answers, she's going to have to ask somebody else, and she knows exactly who.

Rubie crosses to the door, clicking her fingers so the dogs follow her. Before she steps out onto the landing she looks back. The duvet mound hasn't moved. *Well, she can stay there and fester*, thinks Rubie. Taking the hidden key from the top of the door frame, she locks Scarlet in their bedroom and follows Oak and Elm downstairs.

After pulling on her coat and wellies and settling the dogs in their beds in the kitchen, Rubie heads out in the rain, clutching the note that came with the roses inside her pocket. She thought about putting make-up on before she left the house, just in case the mysterious Fenix really is Felton, but then realised it was pointless. If he didn't want her when she was young and beautiful, he's certainly not going to want her now that she's old and scarred. Besides, the only make-up she still owns is well past its use-by date, just like her. She would have probably ended up looking even more grotesque than she already does.

Rubie slows as she approaches the church, her stomach flip-flopping with nerves and anticipation and expectation. While walking here, she raked over everything again, examining it all with the fresh knowledge she now possesses, and has again reached the conclusion that this Fenix character *must* be Felton Clifton. Now that she's geared herself up to see him, the disappointment of not setting eyes on him will surely crush her. She's been wondering and daydreaming and fantasising for two decades and those flimsy pastimes just won't sustain her anymore. She *needs* to see him, to speak to him face to face, dignity be damned.

There's a lone car parked near the entrance to the graveyard, and she can see two people standing on the path. She creeps closer, using the car for cover, before ducking behind the low stone wall.

The rain is coming down heavily now, but Rubie slowly raises her head, just enough to peer over the wall. The two people are directly in her line of sight, although still a fair distance away. They're facing each other and both are slim-built. One is wearing a coat with a hood and the taller one is wearing a dark jacket and a hat. Rubie needs to get a better look at them.

She scoots around the wall to the other side of the church and enters the graveyard via the smaller side path. Passing the bell tower, which sits further back, she scurries to the edge of the external church wall, remaining concealed due to its wider projection. Taking a deep breath, she closes her eyes and psyches herself up, mentally preparing herself for whatever she's about to face or find out or remain frustrated by.

Then, just as she's about to peek, their conversation carries over to her.

'You know, you always used to tell me how cruel Rubie was to you. Seems she's rubbed off on you. Or maybe you're just more like her than you thought.'

Rubie's heart kick-starts, pounding wildly. She knows that voice.

'There's the Felton I know,' says the other person in response.

Rubie clamps her hands over her mouth to suppress her sob. No, it can't be. It can't really be both of them, can it? She shakes her head in disbelief, the knowledge nearly overwhelming her, but she knows she needs to look, to see them with her own eyes. She finally peers around the corner of the church and there they are, right in front of her. Older, different, but still recognisable to her.

Felton and Rosalie.

CHAPTER TWENTY-EIGHT

ALLIE

Felton and I glower at each other. I can see that my words have hurt him and I'm glad. He deserves to die a slow, painful death for what he did to me. To wither into a skeletal husk of himself, hollow-eyed and full of regret. But as we stand-off in this graveyard, in this heavy rain, the pathetic, grovelling, broken man before me seems to rediscover his backbone. He pulls himself up and stands a little straighter.

'You know, you always used to tell me how cruel Rubie was to you. Seems she's rubbed off on you. Or maybe you're just more like her than you thought.'

I huff out a breath, surprised yet not surprised that he's already resorting to cutting comments like that.

'There's the Felton I know,' I say.

'I go by Fenix now,' he retorts, and I snort.

'Phoenix?' I repeat, incredulous. 'Like the bird?'

He tilts his head back and has the audacity to look down his nose at me. 'Different spelling but yes. It's a symbol of my metamorphosis. I became someone new.'

I shake my head. *Metamorphosis?* Is he for real?

'You think you get to be reborn?' I hiss. 'You think you can just change your name and detach yourself from what you did, what you are? Well, you can't. You're still him. You'll always be him deep down. The man who took what he wanted because he could. So don't think you're different now that you've "risen" from the ashes of your depraved actions. You don't get to do that. You don't get to rewrite the past, Felton Clifton. You *raped* me. Violently. You're a rapist!'

His mouth twitches as I speak then he lowers his head and stares at the ground. His beanie hat is drenched, his coat saturated. He nods.

'You're right. I'm a rapist,' he says, his voice barely above a whisper. The words send a chill down my spine. He raises his head and looks me in the eye, his face a dismal mask of despair. 'I wanted you, but you didn't want me, not in that way... But I did it anyway. I raped you. It's unforgivable, I know, but I'm sorry.'

There it is. The bald admission and apology I've waited over two decades to hear. I always thought that if this moment ever came, I'd feel like I could finally fully exhale, that I'd at long last feel free. But there's no release. No relief. If anything, the leaden ache that I've carried with me all this time only feels heavier.

His shoulders sag and he swipes at his face, but I can't tell if it's tears or raindrops he's wiping away. Regardless, I don't believe his reformed, remorseful act for a second.

'Did you at least like the flowers?' he asks.

Flowers? I scrunch my face up, bewildered. What the fuck is he talking about?

'I left them at the farmhouse,' he says. 'With the note.'

The very thought of that place makes me shudder and the fact that he went back to that house with flowers is a sick joke. But then again, it's widely known that criminals like to revisit scenes of their crime and romanticise the experience, or simply revel in it, reliving every last depraved detail. I'm still angry at myself for not seeing his true nature straight away, but I've also learned to give myself grace over the years – I was just a sixteen-year-old grieving for her father, caring for her mother and being bullied by her sisters. Thinking of them, there's a question I need to ask him.

'Did you attack Rubie and Scarlet after you attacked me?' I bark at him.

He jerks his head up. 'No!' he says, vehemently. 'No, I swear that wasn't me. They left the party before me. I was with Colton all night. Phil Roberts was with us for most of it too.'

'How convenient that you and your brother and your mate were each other's alibis,' I say sarcastically.

'It's true. The police would have arrested us if they thought any of us had anything to do with the attack.'

'The police didn't arrest you after you attacked me,' I shoot back.

He nods sadly. 'I know. Thank you.'

Fresh rage fires within me. 'Don't you dare thank me. I had my reasons for not reporting it.' I clench my jaw so hard it hurts as I consider what to do, or say, next.

On the one hand, I don't want to spend another second in the vicinity of this excuse for a man who nearly destroyed my life. I want to walk away and go home to Leeds, safe in the knowledge that karma has already delivered its comeuppance in the form of cancer. On the other hand, I want him to understand the full extent of his actions, of the living and breathing and heartbreaking consequences I was forced to bear. I really want to stick the knife in, make him understand that a pathetic "sorry" just won't cut it. I want what I've always wanted: closure on my terms.

CHAPTER TWENTY-NINE

FENIX

'What reasons?' he asks. 'Why didn't you report me?' He's desperate to know; this is something he's thought about often. He understands how heavy-handed he'd been in the barn that night and the shame of it suffocates him. He really hadn't meant to be like that, not with her, but she was so tempting and once he'd got worked up, he just couldn't control himself. He'd still been much gentler with her than the others, but he supposes she wouldn't have known that, couldn't have known that he'd exercised *some* restraint.

'Don't flatter yourself,' she snarls.

'Flatter myself? No, I don't mean...' He shakes his head. This is not going the way he imagined it would go. He assumed she wouldn't immediately forgive him, and he had braced himself for some hostility, but she's not thawing at all. Can't she see how sincere he is? Doesn't she have any sympathy for a dying man trying to right his wrong?

Movement catches his eye, and he squints beyond Allie, at a figure entering the graveyard. Great, an interruption at the worst possible time. He knows Rosalie – Allie – won't agree to go somewhere else to talk. This is his one and only chance to get her to listen to him, to convince her he deserves to be granted forgiveness. He steps forward and reaches out for her arm, wanting to guide her off the path in order to continue their conversation and prevent the other person from walking closely by them.

'Don't you dare touch me!' she hisses, jerking out of his reach as though his touch could brand her. In a way it already has.

'I'm sorry,' he says hurriedly, holding his palms up, but her reaction hurts. The figure hasn't veered off to one of the graves and is getting closer now, appearing to be heading straight for them. There's something familiar about them. They take a few more steps and then come to a deliberate stop behind Rosalie. Fenix finally sees their face beneath their hood, and it's set with a determined expression. He raises his eyebrows in surprise.

'What are you doing here?' he asks.

CHAPTER THIRTY

ALLIE

I sense someone approaching at the same time as Felton's gaze flicks behind me. For a split-second, I wonder if his brother, Colton, has been waiting in the wings, biding his time as backup. If somehow, on this twentieth anniversary of my sisters' attack, they've orchestrated this supposed chance meeting and intend to do me more harm, and Felton's show of surprise is to throw me off. I'm a fool for ever coming back here. A sitting duck.

I spin around, my body tense but ready to lash out or run if necessary. But the person standing before me on the path isn't Colton Clifton. It's Rye.

My breath catches in my throat as he stares at me, ignoring Felton's question about what he's doing here. His eyes are wide, filled with a range of conflicting emotions... confusion, recognition, sadness?

'Allie,' he whispers, taking another step closer, his hands clenching and unclenching at his sides. He looks so young, so vulnerable. 'I need to ask you something.'

'Did you follow me here?' I retort.

He nods. 'From the B&B. I've chickened out of knocking on

your door a couple of times. I saw you leaving and I need to ask you something,' he repeats.

'Okay.' I shrug, baffled by this turn of events yet thankful for the interruption. I'm also relieved that Rye isn't Felton's brother or one of his other mates from back in the day, here for a sinister reunion. Although, having now met the gnarly Phillip Roberts, I know his physical presence here would not have intimidated me. Colton might have been a different matter though; I remember the rumours about him.

'I know the truth,' Rye says, his voice firmer now.

I blink, back in the moment. The truth? What is he even talking about? 'That's not a question,' I reply obtusely.

'I saw the photo in your room. On the mirror.'

My blood seems to freeze in my veins. 'What?' I say, the word barely audible. Now he has my full attention. I knew he must have been the one who moved it.

Rye's breathing is shallow, his eyes intense. I'm hyper-aware of Felton standing behind me, listening. He's the last person on earth I want hearing whatever Rye's got to say about that precious photo, but I'm a statue; my feet are rooted to the ground, and I feel paralysed.

'Mum has the same photo. I remembered it. I found it.' He swallows, struggling to articulate himself. 'The necklace – you're wearing the same one today.'

My brain is racing ten steps ahead. I instinctively touch the locket hanging around my neck. My mum's necklace. I curl my fingers around it protectively in a futile attempt to hide it from him, from the truth I now realise he's clearly pieced together and is about to reveal.

'You're the one holding the baby, aren't you? And I'm the baby. You're...' His voice cracks, his expression a combination of anger and acceptance. 'You're my mother. My real mum.'

There's the question he wanted to ask. The solid ground

beneath me seems to tilt and my head swims. I feel like I'm going to faint. Rye is my son – the baby I gave up? My chest burns with panic as I look at him, really look at him. And suddenly I wonder why I hadn't seen it before. Maybe I had but like everything else, I just pushed it down, blocked it out. He has my eyes, my original cheekbones before my treatments. His hood is up now but a few dark-red strands of hair are plastered to his forehead, the same colour as his father's was.

What's happening here? First Felton and now Rye. All of us here in Stonethorpe-On-Sea, where it all began. It's too much to process and I don't know what to say. I don't know what to feel. Marla's words come back to me: *Ever since we got him.* I realise now she must have meant adoption. She and her husband adopted Rye and brought him up here. What are the chances?

But then I have another thought. What if this is a cruel trick – something Felton's set up to manipulate me? My brain feels like mush yet the sharpest it's ever been at the same time, vacillating between past and present, considering myriad options and outcomes, all of them able to send shockwaves through my carefully curated life. I didn't ask for this, I didn't expect any of this to happen. I need to buy myself some time to think, to talk to Rye properly, away from Felton.

But just as I'm about to speak, Felton asks an explosive question that catches me further off guard.

'You got pregnant, Rosalie?'

'Shut up!' I shout at him. 'You don't get to ask me that.'

'Rosalie?' asks Rye. 'You're Rosalie Sanderson?' He shakes his head. 'Did you come back to find me?'

'Please tell me,' begs Felton, and I clamp my hands over my ears and close my eyes, too overwhelmed to answer either of them.

'Stop, both of you!' I cry.

Suddenly I feel arms wrapped around me, like a straitjacket. I scream, jerking my body, throwing them off.

'Hey, get off her!' I hear Rye's voice and open my eyes. In a swoosh of movement he lunges towards Felton, who has hold of me. His fist is clenched and raised, his face twisted and determined. He throws a punch, which Felton dodges, but he lets go of me and they both go down and begin grappling on the path.

'Rye, it's okay, I'm okay!' I try to grab his arm to pull him back but he's too strong, too intent on protecting me. He didn't need me to answer his question; he already knows.

'Rye, please stop!' I shout. 'He's got cancer.' As much as I'd love to see Felton Clifton dead, I don't want it to be like this, for Rye to have to live with the aftermath and consequences of killing him. Maybe I am capable of thinking like a mother.

My words finally register and Rye scrambles up. He stands, panting, while Felton peels himself off the soaked path.

'He was hurting you,' says Rye, his harsh tone at odds with his kind reasoning. He looks ashamed of himself yet also proud, and I wonder if that was his first-ever fight. If it was, I feel strangely grateful at least I got to witness one milestone in his life.

'He wasn't.' I smile sadly. 'He can't anymore.'

'Who is he anyway?' he asks, flicking a withering glance at Felton.

I consider my answer. I don't want to tell him, but I owe him the truth.

'He's your father,' I say.

23RD OCTOBER 1997

CHAPTER THIRTY-ONE

ROSALIE

The barn is so quiet and peaceful. It feels like a different planet compared to the constant chaos of the house, plus I like the fact that Dad's oak tree is close by. I always come here when I need to escape, when even my bedroom offers no privacy from the nebby noses of my invasive sisters. Mum won't let me lock my door, so they just barge in whenever they want, whenever they're bored, which is most of the time. I'd be bored if I had their personalities too. Their cutting remarks from earlier echo around my head.

'Just fuck off and read one of your books or something, Rosalie, you creepy little mouse,' Rubie had snapped after accusing me of spying on her and Scarlet giving each other one of their frequent "makeovers" as they "tested looks" ahead of Kayleigh's party on Sunday. As if I'd ever want make-up tips from them and their "more is more" mentality. More blush, more gloss, more sass.

Scarlet, as always, had backed Rubie up instantly, snorting at her comment. 'Honestly, Rube, she's probably reading those steamy romance novels, getting her kicks from books because she'll never get them in real life.'

I cut off their bitchy cackles by slamming their bedroom door, but their insults had stayed with me. So much so, I needed to come to the barn, my sanctuary, to get away from them properly. I thought that after losing Dad we might learn how to get along, but his stark absence, and Mum struggling with her MS, and surly Uncle Silas visiting more often has only widened the wedge between me and them.

Crossing my legs, I lean against a bale of hay with my book open on my knees. It's not a steamy romance as Scarlet scoffed at but a VC Andrews novel I borrowed from the mobile library. I need to read as widely as I can if I want to do an English literature degree one day. The thought of leaving Mum to go to university makes me sad but she's always encouraging me to go for it. She says it would be a crime to waste my brain.

The barn smells musty and earthy but it's grounding and familiar. I breathe it in, attempting to calm my frazzled nervous system as I try to lose myself in the sinister story of the Dollanganger siblings. But I still can't concentrate on the pages in front of me thanks to my sisters' mocking faces swooshing smack bang in the middle of my mind's eye, chanting their cruel names for me, repeating their cruellest insults to me.

It's not just their nastiness that bothers me though, it's the way they make me feel within this now fractured family. Being a triplet isn't as special as people think it is, and being an identical triplet is worse. Always seeing the other two staring back whenever you look in a mirror and constantly being surrounded by two other versions of yourself as though you've been cloned. It's freaky and actually messes with your mind.

A sound from outside snaps me out of my glum and familiar train of thought. I'm instantly on high alert, wondering if one or both of them have come to invade my peace and taunt me further. But after a few moments, no one appears in the doorway of the barn, and I breathe a sigh of relief.

Settling back against the hay bale, I consciously guide my thoughts in a different direction, towards my biggest secret: Felton Clifton. I think about his crooked grin and dark-red hair and strong, muscly arms. He's so different to his friends and his brother – the loud, brash boys who think catcalling girls is attractive. Felton is quieter, brooding, always ready to listen. He really makes me feel heard. And seen. He makes me feel unique and not like I'm just one of the three interchangeable Sanderson sisters.

I was wary of him at first. The Clifton boys have quite the reputation in town. Most state that they're troublemakers. Some whisper they're worse than that, criminals even, the same as their father, but the family's caravan park is good for tourism. So blind eyes are often turned, apparently. I prefer not to listen to hearsay and to judge people on their actual behaviour, and Felton has never been anything but sweet to me.

He kissed me for the first time last week, on the same sand dunes where we first crossed paths earlier in the summer. He was so gentle and respectful, nothing like the rumours I'd heard. Afterwards, he looked at me with such affection in his eyes that I swore my heart skipped a beat.

I sigh, finally admitting to myself that I'm too wired to read tonight. I close my book and set it down beside me before closing my eyes and leaning my head back. An owl hoots in the distance, and I shiver slightly, not quite warm enough in just my jeans and long-sleeved T-shirt. But I'm too settled to move, and I don't want to go back in the house yet, back to my hideous sisters. If only they could see me the way Felton does, understand that just because I like different things to them and get more joy from art and books and animals than clothes and make-up and boy bands, it doesn't make me inferior. When they're not treating me like the odd one out, they act like I'm invisible, actively refusing to acknowledge my questions or even my presence at times. Sometimes I think about cutting my hair off, severing the long, black, silky strands that we've all been born with, but the one time I voiced this thought, Mum was distraught.

'But you girls all have the most beautiful princess hair, Rosalie. It's your crowning glory. I'd be so sad if you had it cut. Promise me you won't?'

And I can't upset her, not now. Her illness is getting worse; her hacking coughs echo through the house when Rubie and Scarlet haven't got their boy band music blasting on the highest volume. I'll wait, for now. But as soon as she starts getting better, I'm doing it, I'm getting a Rachel cut – she's my favourite character from *Friends* and I love her individuality.

'Rosalie?'

His voice startles me. I open my eyes and jerk my head up to see Felton Clifton standing in the doorway of the barn, silhouetted against the fading sunlight, looking sheepish and sexy.

I sit up straighter, trying my best to hide my shock. I'm surprised but happy to see him. 'Felton? What are you doing here?'

He steps towards me, his grin playful.

'I was going to be romantic and throw stones at your bedroom window then I realised I didn't know which one was your bedroom.'

I laugh. 'So what... you thought you'd look for me in the barn?'

'No, I sat on the wall and waited for a light to come on upstairs, hoping to see you, but I only saw your sisters. Then I watched you come in here. I waited some more until I knew you were alone.'

'That sounds like stalker behaviour,' I say, attempting to sound stern, but I'm not. I'm thrilled that he's here.

He's right in front of me now and he crouches down, his eyes boring into mine. 'What can I say? You're worth the wait. But I'll go if you don't want me to stay.'

I can lie when necessary but there's no need to pretend with him, no need to act coy.

I smile. 'I want you to stay. I'll be glad of some good company for a change.'

He moves to sit beside me, so close that I can feel the warmth of him. He stretches his long legs out, crosses them at the ankles. He smells so good.

'So why are you hiding out here?' he asks. 'Sister trouble again?'

'How did you guess?' I hesitate, conscious that I complain about my sisters a lot, but the words just spill out. 'They just... they always make me feel so... inconsequential to them. Like I'm an annoying insect in the summer of their lives.'

'How poetic,' he says, grinning again.

I swat him on the arm playfully and he laughs, catching my wrist. He places my hand on top of his and intertwines our fingers. He kisses my knuckles gently.

'They're jealous of you,' he tells me, after a minute.

I huff out a breath. 'Jealous? Yeah, right. Of what?'

He reaches out and cups my face, rubbing his thumb along my cheek. 'Of this,' he says softly.

I roll my eyes. 'It's the same as theirs.'

'It's not. Nor this.' He twirls a lock of my hair around his finger. 'You're an elevation of them, on a higher level of your own. Anyone with eyes can see that. Don't ever change.'

'What if I want to change? I was actually thinking about cutting my hair,' I say.

'Don't,' he says, gently tugging on the strands he's holding, pulling me closer. Before I know it, he's kissing me.

I let him. I welcome it. His lips are soft, his movements unhurried and the flutters in my stomach intensify rapidly. He shifts, bringing one of his legs over both of mine and our kisses deepen. But when he hooks an arm around my waist and manoeuvres me into a lying position, pressing his body on top of mine, I murmur his name and ask him to stop. A relatively chaste kiss on the dunes is one thing, but this feels like it could turn into something else, and I realise now I'm not ready for that. I want to go slow.

'It's okay, Rosalie,' he says, nestling into my neck, pulling my T-shirt to the side to plant kisses along my collarbone before clamping his mouth back on mine.

The weight of him feels suffocating and panic starts to set in. I twist my face away from his, trying to breathe evenly, to stay calm. What I'm suddenly afraid is going to happen can't actually happen, can it?

'Felton, please stop,' I say again, unable to disguise the tremor in my voice.

And then his hands are everywhere, no longer gentle. He rakes his gaze over my body, no longer appreciative but primal, dangerous.

'Tell me you want me,' he says.

I shake my head, press my lips together in an act of defiance. In a split-second everything has changed.

He squeezes my cheeks together, making my lips pucker like a fish's mouth.

'Tell me you want me,' he repeats through gritted teeth while pulling open the fly of his jeans.

I realise now I have no choice. I whisper the lie, 'I want you.'

He smiles and I turn my head to the side, unable to look at him anymore.

He turns me over as easily as if I was one of the dolls my sisters and I used to play with when we were children. He yanks my jeans and knickers down. And then he does what he probably planned on doing all along while holding the back of my head and squashing the side of my face into the hay-strewn ground. I make myself go limp, disassociate from the act, stare blankly at the steel hoof cutter hanging next to Maple's old saddle and reins. And then something catches my eye. Through my watery vision, I see her. Scarlet. She's standing in the barn doorway, a strange expression on her face. Fascination, maybe, weirdly. For a moment I think she's going to do something, anything, to help me, but then I blink and she's gone.

My ordeal only lasts a few minutes. Afterwards, Felton pulls up my knickers and jeans, then he holds out a hand to help me up. Bizarrely, I let him. He buttons himself up as casually as if this was our hundredth lovers' fumble in the barn, not a non-consensual criminal incident. He guides me to sit on one of the hay bales then leans down and kisses me softly on my forehead.

'You're amazing, Rosalie,' he says, as if we've just shared something beautiful.

I don't move. I don't look at him. I notice my book on the floor and know that I'll never be able to finish it now. I'll never be able to look at *Flowers in the Attic* ever again without thinking of Felton Clifton and this night, and this barn, and of what he just did to me.

'Catch you later,' he says.

In my peripheral vision I see him salute as he walks out, humming contentedly.

I sit here, on this hay bale, for what feels like hours. Scarlet doesn't come back. Nobody comes to check on me. Nobody cares. I'm cold and my body aches but still I sit, my mind spinning with a whole host of turbulent emotions: shock, shame, sadness, anger.

Eventually, I get up and go inside, intent on only one thing. The house sleeps as I rummage in the chest of drawers in the front living room until I find my mum's sewing kit tin. I creep upstairs and lock myself in the bathroom with it. I take out the dressmaker's scissors, stand in front of the mirror, grab a handful of my hair, and cut.

24TH OCTOBER 1997
SCARLET

OMG she's actually gone and done it! Rosalie has chopped her hair off! I can't believe it. A right mess she's made of it too. We didn't even know until tonight. Rubie barged into her bedroom, called her a lazy sloth for lying in bed all day and yanked back her duvet. That's when we saw the new hairdo! Rubie started laughing hysterically, she had tears in her eyes and everything. She said Rosie looked like Wayne from Wayne's World *and started singing the theme song to her! Rosie went mental, more ballistic than I've ever seen her, screaming at her to get out. Her face was all red and blotchy and her eyes were bulging loads just like those fish with the googly eyes.*

Mum actually cried when she saw Rosie, which made Rubie laugh even more, like an evil hyena. At that point I thought it was actually a bit sad but had to pretend it was hilarious or else Rubie would have started on me too. I don't know what made Rosalie want to do it. The whole thing was quite weird considering what she got up to last night. I would have thought she'd have been in a better mood. Maybe FC wasn't that great in the sack... or should I say hay! Maybe she wanted to give herself a new look for turning seventeen and didn't mean to cut that much off. I bet she kept getting the sides uneven! Whatever, she really does look as ugly as sin now! I'm never cutting my hair if it's going to make me look that bad. It has made me want to cut Rubie's hair off while she's asleep though... and then I'd be the only pretty one left. It'd serve her right for being such a bitch to me all our lives. Do you think she'd be mad if I did it? Why am I even asking because I know the answer... she'd literally kill me with the same scissors! Still... it's really tempting.

CHAPTER THIRTY-TWO

RUBIE

Still hidden behind the church wall, Rubie seethes as Rosalie attacks Felton with her acidic words. Apparently, she told him Rubie was a cruel bitch when they were younger. She's one to talk. Rubie decides she can't listen to any more of Rosalie's ire and is just about to step out, to make herself known, to stand in support of Felton, when someone else enters the graveyard and stops behind Rosalie on the path. She narrows her eyes at the interloper, a young man with dark-red hair. He addresses Rosalie.

'Allie, I need to ask you something.'

Allie? Who the hell is Allie? And then it clicks: Allie is short for Rosalie.

As Rubie continues to watch, things suddenly take a turn, and the young man hurls himself at Felton and they begin scuffling on the ground. Rubie judders in shock, wanting to intervene but unwilling to make herself known in the middle of whatever this is. It's been a long time since she's been in such close proximity to any men other than Uncle Silas and seeing a fight break out in front of her has thrown her. Rubie's heart immediately goes out to Felton, who is struggling to fend off the younger man. She turns her face away, unable to bear simply watching from the sidelines for another second, especially as Rosalie is being a useless referee right in the midst of it. Then she hears Rosalie shout something outrageous.

'He's got cancer!'

Rubie swivels her head back towards the savage scene, stunned. Tears well in her eyes as the young man ceases his attack and stands back looking sheepish while Felton struggles to get back up. Rubie wants to rage on his behalf, condemn their cruel treatment of him regardless, never mind that he's a cancer patient. She goes inside herself, absorbing the information, trying to process the news. Another of life's cruel outcomes: she may have finally got the chance to reunite with her teenage love but he's dying? How inexplicably tragic. Then, just as she thinks things can't possibly get any worse, Rosalie says three words that cause Rubie's head to spin.

'He's your father.'

Rubie can't believe her ears. She feels like she's been kicked in the stomach. Felton and Rosalie have a son? And Rosalie kept it a secret and now she's claiming he forced himself on her, even though Scarlet saw them at it. Scarlet may have been a sneaky little bitch of a sister, but she wouldn't have ignored rape!

Rubie is appalled. Of course Rosalie would twist the story to make herself the victim. And no wonder she's good at it – she spent most of their childhood with her nose either stuck in a book or stuck in the air believing she was better than Rubie and Scarlet. Every word that she's heard drip from her long-lost sister's mouth has poured acid into the festering wound that she's been frequently picking at for two decades. No, there's no way that night in the barn was rape. Every girl in town wanted Felton, and Rosalie wouldn't have been the exception. But she got herself knocked up and chose to run away rather than explain herself to their mother and Uncle Silas, who would have both burned with the shame of her teenage pregnancy. Yet Rubie is insane with jealousy that her sister got to bear Felton's child, got everything that she herself wanted.

Rubie digs her fingernails into the soft flesh of her palms, but the pain is dull in comparison to her internal agony. Her heart goes out to Felton, again, this man she wanted so desperately, the man she thought would whisk her away from sorry old Stonethorpe-On-Sea. But that's not what happened.

After the attack, she never got the chance to speak to him ever again. Not that she wanted to, looking like the bride of Frankenstein. And he was probably warned to keep his distance from their family after being questioned by the police. But she wonders now, in the light of knowing that Scarlet kept secrets from her, if he had ever dared knock on their door years ago, before he left town. Maybe Scarlet saw him or heard him asking to see Rubie, not Rosalie. Maybe Silas sent him packing then too. Maybe she missed her chance back then.

Rubie takes a fortifying breath. It's time. She steps forward, finally revealing herself to the twisted trio. Her heart pounds painfully and her whole body shakes with rage. The years of pent-up fury burst out of her, and she screams one word, raw and rage-filled: 'Liar!'

Her voice startles them and they turn to her, shock registering on Rosalie and Felton's faces, surprise on Rye's. Good, let them be shocked.

'You selfish, cowardly bitch of a liar!' she shouts, taking another step towards Rosalie, her fists clenched at her sides. 'You ruined everything for me and Scarlet and now you have the cheek to come back and act like some sort of victim? Like you deserve sympathy?'

Rosalie – or Allie as she calls herself now – swallows but stands stock still, her altered face pale beneath her hood. Fenix – Felton – is also frozen, gaunt and slim. The young man – Rye – steps back wearing a bewildered expression, almost losing his footing on the soggy grass.

'You took everything from me – Felton and Mum!' Rubie swings her arms wide to encompass her losses. Her voice cracks but she doesn't stop. She's waited a long time to get all this out and she's not going to stop now.

'Do you know how much worry you caused after you ran away and played dead? Mum's darling Rosalie, her angel who could do no wrong. All the pain and grief and abuse we've endured for *twenty* years? We've all suffered, Rosalie. But now here you are again. The little mouse with a tall tale of your own – that Felton raped you. That he's a bad guy. Well, Scarlet knows otherwise. She saw you screwing him! Why do you want to destroy his life too?'

Tears burn behind Rubie's eyes, but she blinks them away, refusing to let them spill down her cheeks. She won't give Rosalie the satisfaction of seeing her cry.

Rosalie doesn't respond but her eyes are locked on Rubie's. For a moment, Rubie considers lashing out, wanting to make her feel even a fraction of the pain she's lived with, that she currently feels. Her estranged sister's expression is unreadable, reminding Rubie of Scarlet's frequent blankness. She comes to the conclusion that they're both dead inside.

Rubie moves her gaze to Felton for the first time and isn't surprised to find a look of pity on his face following her honest outburst. This skinny man, so far removed from the strapping hunk he once was, this cancer-ridden shadow of his former self pities *her*. She's pathetic.

'Why did you want her more than me?' she asks, her desire for the answer greater than her shame for asking it.

Felton shrugs. A dismissive gesture. The pitiful look has gone, replaced by something harder.

'You were too easy,' he admits.

His bald admission is another punch to her gut. She gapes at him, struggling to recover.

'You were practically begging for it, throwing yourself at me like some "pick me" girl. That doesn't really do it for me. I wanted something different...' He glances at Rosalie. 'Someone with a bit more depth.'

Rubie blinks rapidly, trying again to prevent the tears from coming. 'It wasn't like that,' she says, shaking her head. 'You led me outside to a secluded spot. You kissed me. You said I looked gorgeous.'

Felton sighs. 'Look, I was wasted and horny, and it was a two-minute fumble in the garden. Let's not romanticise it, okay? It was a party, and we had some fun, that's all. Standard stuff for me and my mates back then.'

Rubie glances at Rosalie, embarrassed by Felton's cold, casual summary of what she has convinced herself was a meaningful union. Rosalie has a face like thunder, yet she still doesn't speak.

'No, that's not all. It was special!' protests Rubie.

Felton frowns, impatience now crossing his face. 'Look, I'm not here to rehash the night of the party with you, Rubie. I've got enough to deal with already. This doesn't involve you.'

Rubie gasps. 'Doesn't involve me?' she screeches. 'Are you kidding? That party was the only good time I've had in the past twenty years!' Her vision blurs as she stares at him, her heart breaking. Felton hasn't been thinking about her all this time, too afraid to return to Stonethorpe in case he's questioned again about her attack. He hasn't been biding his time, planning on making amends because their budding romance hadn't been able to blossom properly. She didn't make the lasting impression on him she thought she did, the way he did on her. No, Rosalie was the true object of his affections all along. Now that her fantasy has finally been extinguished, her embroidered memory unpicked, she's got nothing left to lose.

She clenches her fists at her sides and screams, 'I deserved better than you!'

CHAPTER THIRTY-THREE

ALLIE

'No, I deserved better than both of you!' I scream, every ounce of hatred I've been holding on to for the past twenty years wrapped around my words like barbed wire. I want them to cut Rubie and Felton, to puncture them and make them bleed.

I turn to Rubie. My throat is raw and I'm trembling with adrenaline, but I need to say this, I need to get it out. 'I know Scarlet saw us in the barn. She stood and watched him raping me and then she just left.' I feel my bottom lip wobble, but I refuse to let myself cry. I power on, my voice cracking with emotion. 'And I know she told you because you always told each other everything. But neither of you helped me or checked on me afterwards. Not that night, not the next day even though I'd hacked all my fucking hair off, and not a few days later when you went to Kayleigh's party. Then you even had sex with him there!' I point at Felton, throwing him a look of disgust. 'And I already knew that back then because I heard you telling Scarlet all about it, how "mind-blowing" it was. But now it sounds like he didn't rate you as highly as you told her he did.' I laugh nastily.

Rubie shakes her head, her jaw clenched. 'You're

211

delusional! You couldn't have heard me telling Scarlet about it,' she retorts. Even though twenty years have passed, she sounds exactly like she used to when we were teenagers, her tone bitchy and superior. 'I only told her while we were walking home, just before we got attacked. You were at home in bed then, little mouse.'

Her derogatory old nickname for me enrages me. But I let it soak in, savouring the moment, knowing exactly what I'm going to say next.

I slowly smirk at her. 'I was there,' I say. I fix my stare on her and wait for her to figure it out.

The penny finally drops, and Rubie raises a shaking finger, pointing at me. Her mouth opens and closes like a blobfish. Her wet hair is plastered to her head, barely covering her angry scar.

'It was you.' She lets out an anguished cry, disbelief quickly giving way to realisation.

'It was me.' The debut confession tastes bitter on my tongue but it's also a relief to finally say it out loud. 'I attacked you and Scarlet that night.'

To my right, Rye sucks in a shocked breath.

'What the fuck?' cries Felton.

'But why?' asks Rubie in a pitiful tone. It reminds me of when we were little and her standard response to our mum's repeated, whispered requests for her and Scarlet to let me play with them too.

I smile sweetly, feeling high on the honesty. Is this why people confess their sins to priests – to get this rush? 'When you were getting ready for the party, I heard you bitching about me to Scarlet, as usual, and then fantasising about Felton. How do you think I felt knowing my own sister was planning to have sex with my rapist? And that my other sister was encouraging it, despite what she knew he had done to me! The only thing I regret is not finishing you both off properly,' I add cruelly, rubbing salt into the raw wound.

Rubie suddenly snaps out of her stupefied state. She launches herself at me like a wild animal, teeth bared, emitting a guttural scream that echoes around the graveyard. Her nails make contact with my neck, gouging my skin, and I yelp. I manage to push her off, but she scrambles straight back up. This time I'm ready. I've been ready for this rematch for years.

We collide with a force that knocks us both off balance and we crash onto the grass, grappling, shoving, scratching, thrashing. I'm vaguely aware of Rye trying to separate us but our deep-seated anger and hatred of one another keeps us bound together, finally united in one common purpose: to overthrow the other. Will this be a fight to the death? I grab her hair, still long but now stringy rather than lustrous, and yank her head back, her scarred cheek close to my face. It really is a deep gouge, an ugly, puckered, permanent deformation. I feel absolutely no remorse.

Somehow, she twists and jabs me just below my ribcage. I pull my knees up and she rolls off me onto the other side of the path. Rye is panting beside me, and I realise he must have pushed her. He holds out a hand to pull me up and I take it gratefully. Rubie is now on her feet too, wiping blood as red as her name from her cut lip.

'You hated us that much?' she asks, flapping her arms against her sides. She reminds me of a penguin with her black hair and white face and dark clothes, and I laugh.

This clearly riles her as she comes at me again, swinging wildly. I manage to sidestep her but she's relentless and moves quickly, grabbing at my coat. The grass is slippery, and I almost fall as I twist away but a headstone helps me stay upright. I propel myself off it only to see Rubie taking off, weaving through the graves. Rye jerks forward, as if to chase after her but

I don't want him to. I want to catch her myself. I shake my head at him and take off. She's slow, lumbering, not the lithe little nymph she once was, and I close the distance between us easily.

I hear Felton shout my name – my old name – and it all comes flooding back again. That night. That degrading, hideous encounter in the barn that Scarlet witnessed yet chose to ignore. I know in my bones that she told Rubie. They never kept secrets from each other; it was always me that was the odd one out. The loathing I feel for them, will forever feel about them, consumes me like a black fog.

With a burst of energy I make contact, shoving Rubie hard in the back. She shrieks in surprise and stumbles forward, falling face first against the headstone of our mother's grave. The sickening crack makes me grimace. She slides to the ground like liquid.

For a moment I stand there, breathing hard, staring at her limp form, her bloodied, bashed-in head. I'm aware of Rye appearing by my side.

'Fuck,' he says, succinctly.

I step closer, the adrenaline still fizzing within me, and look down at my sister. Kneeling, I reach out, stroke the blood-soaked hair back from her forehead, regard the face which used to be so like my own but now is just saggy and scarred and severe.

'Happy birthday, Rubie,' I whisper.

'We need to call an ambulance.' Felton's voice makes me jump. I had forgotten he was there, watching the drama from the wings, silent and sullen. I bet he was getting off on seeing two sisters catfighting.

'Rye,' he calls out, his voice desperate now. 'Help me! We need to put her in the recovery position.'

Rye looks at me, waiting for my instruction, already showing unconditional loyalty. Rather than regarding this as an attempt at murder, he's showing he's got my back. I feel a stab of what could perhaps be maternal affection but is probably just gratitude to have a ready ally in this bizarre, traumatic, unexpected turn of events.

'Wait. Let me think,' I say.

'You just want to leave her to die? Second time lucky, is that it? Why did you ask me if I attacked your sisters when you knew it was you?' asks Felton, incredulous. 'Talk about mind games.'

'You're in no fucking position to judge me,' I say.

Suddenly, a deep, stern voice breaks through the air, jolting us all out of the situation.

'What in God's name is going on here?'

CHAPTER THIRTY-FOUR

ALLIE

I snap my head towards the interloper. The vicar stands at the edge of the graveyard, his face pale with horror, frozen at the end of the path. His concerned, confused gaze flits between Rubie's prone body and Felton, who is standing next to where I'm kneeling. He's arrived back to the church at the worst possible time. Bizarrely, I wonder if I ought to ask to interview him for the book, as Mason suggested, even though he's not the same vicar that was here in the nineties.

'I'm ringing the police,' he calls as he fumbles in his pocket for his phone.

The second he retrieves it and looks down at the screen, I seize my chance. With a burst of adrenaline, I spring up and start running across the graveyard towards the side gate, past the bell tower end of the church.

'Allie, wait!' I hear Rye cry, but I keep going, not looking back. If the vicar summons the police and Felton calls an ambulance, I can't be here when they all arrive. I've managed to outrun my past for twenty years and I want no part of it now. I refuse to revert back to being Rosalie Sanderson in the eyes of the public.

And then I hear the heavy thud of footsteps behind me. I chance a look, and I'm surprised to see Felton, not Rye, chasing me. Of course he is. He always has been. Maybe not physically but emotionally, mentally, he's always been there, haunting my dreams like a malingering presence I could never quite exorcise despite my best efforts.

But I'm stronger and fitter than him now and I will not allow him to ensnare me or overpower me. I pound my feet on top of the uneven ground, occasionally slipping on the wet grass and remnants of soggy, dying flowers that have been left on top of the graves. I feel bad for trampling over them, and for disturbing the dead lying below, but I can't let him catch me, put his hands on me, ever again.

And then I stumble, twisting my ankle awkwardly. I let out a cry and fall forward, sliding painfully onto a patch of sloppy mud beside a freshly dug grave. I try to scramble up, but a hot poker of pain shoots up my leg. I realise that Felton has grabbed me from behind.

'Let me go!' I yell, trying to kick out and twist my body, anything to break free. He's surprisingly strong for a dying man and manages to cling on to the hem of my soaked jeans.

'Allie, please just stop!' His voice is desperate but not pathetic and his manhandling of me reminds me of that night. It sends a fresh shockwave of rage through me, and I realise I'm not sixteen anymore. I'm not weak or pliable or indefensible and I'm not trapped in a barn with him, terrified into submission, manipulated into place like a doll. I'm older and angrier than I've ever been. And this is the moment I've been waiting for. It takes effort but I manage to yank down my zip then contort my arm to my coat's inner pocket, fumbling for the small can of rape spray I always carry with me, just in case. I twist sharply, kicking out and turning over onto my back to face him, enjoying the split-second of confusion in his eyes. Before he can move, I press down hard on the trigger and a stream of burning liquid shoots him square in the eyes.

He lets out the most wretched scream and presses his palms against his face, staggering unsteadily, disorientated and distressed. I leap up and push him hard, sending him to the ground square on his tailbone. He cries out again and his hands automatically leave his now red and burning face, enabling him to crab walk backwards away from me. But he goes too far, too fast, managing to gain good purchase on the wet ground. I pant, anticipating the probable outcome yet doing nothing to warn him. Seconds later, I watch in fascinated horror as he scrambles ungainly towards the edge of the open grave. His left wrist pushes against the edge and as it gives way, he screeches in shock before desperately trying to prevent the inevitable by jerking his head forwards, trying somehow to prevent gravity from doing what gravity does. Of course, he doesn't manage it and he slips into the open grave, head and shoulders first, as though descending a vertical mudslide to hell.

I gasp and look around for Rye, suddenly wanting him next to me, and he's already there, his eyes wide with shock.

We slowly step towards the grave and peer down. Felton's head is at an unnatural angle to his head. His neck looks broken, and his glassy eyes stare back at us.

'I... I... didn't mean for that to happen,' I whisper, although I'm not sure that's true.

Rye's gaze shifts from Felton's crooked body and back to me. 'I know. It was self-defence,' he says. 'I saw him chase you and try to attack you. After we saw him and Rubie arguing and then him push her onto that headstone.' He jerks his thumb back towards my mum's grave. 'He was a dangerous stranger, wasn't he? We didn't know him or his intentions.'

Tears blur my vision as I process his meaningful statement. 'You'd do that, for me?'

He nods without hesitation and gives me a half smile. 'Of course I would. You're my mum.'

Those three words chink the armour I've been wearing for twenty years, just enough to let some of my hardened core seep through, and out of me. I begin to sob, my body shaking, as Rye pulls me into his arms.

I can hear the sirens in the distance. The police, the ambulance, all racing towards us, but for the first time in my life I don't feel completely alone. Rye and I are in this together.

'Are you both all right?' calls the vicar as he navigates his way over, concern etched on his face.

I peek out from Rye's embrace and nod. 'I think we will be now,' I say as the older man reaches us, slightly out of breath from all the excitement and exertion.

'Let's get you out of the rain. Come inside and wait for the cavalry,' he says, ushering us towards the church. His kindness and gentle manner make me want to cry again.

Rye and I let him guide us back to the main entrance where he leaves us to return to Rubie. He kneels down and takes her limp hand in his and I honestly don't know if my sister is dead or alive. But this time I'm not going to take off and leave her. I'm going to stay and give a witness statement to the police and it will be signed *Allie Sawyer*.

Later, Rye and I return to the B&B together and Marla's in an instant flap at the sight of us.

'Look at the pair of you! You're absolutely soaked to the skin and caked in mud!' she says as she hurries us inside. 'Sit yourselves down and I'll make you both some hot chocolate.'

'Yeah, I ran into Allie when I was out and about. We got caught in the downpour and ended up cutting across the field near the church,' explains Rye unnecessarily as he peels off his jacket. Marla takes it straight off him and holds out her hand for mine. It's a touching, maternal gesture and I feel a sudden urge to thank her for taking such good care of my son. But I don't. Rye and I have already agreed on our plan of action.

'I'm going straight in the shower,' I say, worried about my wig dislodging even further when I pull down my hood. I head for the stairs before she can protest.

'Come back down for your drink,' suggests Rye.

I look back at him and nod. 'Give me ten minutes.'

Back in my room I take off my soaked boots, sodden coat and my wet, muddy clothes. I stand in front of the mirror in just my underwear, my long black glossy wig now just skew-whiff slimy tendrils stuck to the side of my face and hanging down my back. This is definitely the last time I will ever wear it. I undo the grips and slide it off, mentally saying goodbye to Rosalie Sanderson for good.

After I have showered and dressed and donned my usual pink hair, I enter the dining room to find Rye already sitting at one of the tables and Marla placing two mugs of hot chocolate in front of him, both with cones of squirty cream and sprinkles on top. I smile at the very childish- but very delicious-looking drinks.

'Served just like my Bruce used to make,' she says as she flicks the electric fire on. 'Come and sit down and warm up, dear.'

I slide onto a seat and cup my hands around the mug, surprised to realise I'm still shaking. The drama must have affected me more than I thought; it's been quite the afternoon.

'Now, I've also taken the liberty of baking a few chocolate chip muffins for your birthday,' announces Marla. 'Plus they're our Rye's favourite.' She ruffles his still-damp hair, and he bats her away, embarrassed. 'They'll be out of the oven any minute. You two enjoy your drinks and I'll be back soon.'

'She's a lovely woman,' I say as soon as Marla has left the room and is out of earshot. 'I'm glad you've got each other.'

Rye smooths his hair back down and I see an echo of the boy he once was in his self-conscious movements. I feel a rush of affection for him.

'When you were born,' I whisper, my voice trembling, knowing this may be my only chance to tell him, 'I called you Charlie.' I pause for a moment, to collect myself. 'It means free and that's what I wanted you to be. Not tethered to me, or your father, for the rest of your life. You deserved a clean slate and not to be a Sanderson or a Clifton.'

Rye smiles, his eyes shining. 'It's still my name. Mum and Dad – Marla and Bruce – kept it the same.'

I smile too, my heart aching with a strange mixture of sorrow and pride. Charlie. My baby. The one thing I couldn't keep has found his way back to me.

We drink our hot chocolates, laughing as we wipe cream off our noses, and a few minutes later, Marla returns bearing the delicious-looking muffins. But rather than wearing a proud expression, she seems flustered.

'I've just had Maeve on the phone. Now, what's all this about the police and an ambulance turning up at the church? She says Father Kiely called them, some altercation or other. Did you two see or hear anything when you were out and about?'

Rye glances at me then turns to his mother. 'Yeah, actually, we were there. It was the weirdest thing,' he begins...

WEDNESDAY 31ST OCTOBER 2018

CHAPTER THIRTY-FIVE

ALLIE

The sunlight is glittering on the surface of the ocean like a million diamonds. The warm breeze carries the crisp, salty tang of the sea and here, on this yacht, I feel myself relax completely for what feels like the first time ever. My bare shoulders are slightly burnt, and my hair tickles the tender skin. It's grown back thicker and healthier over the past year, and I haven't felt the need to wear a wig for months. I do still wear my mum's locket though, the tiny picture of my sisters and I inside, our chubby baby faces identical. It was the only era that we ever were all the same, at least visually.

Mason is below deck somewhere, probably investigating every nook and cranny – forever the curious journalist. I do like that about him, most of the time. Up here on deck it's peaceful, just me and the open, turquoise Mediterranean Sea. And my book. I'm finally reading *Flowers in the Attic*, through to the end for the first time. At its heart it's a dark and poignant story of overcoming oppression despite despicable family circumstances. I wonder if I would have appreciated its themes in the same way when I was sixteen. I doubt it. They say you often read the right book at the right time in your life and that seems to be true. After all, here I am on my thirty-eighth birthday, and I couldn't have wished for a better way to spend it. This time a year ago I was running through a graveyard, fighting my rapist, fighting the past, fighting for my future. And now here I am. Finally free from all the shackles of my old life.

It's strange to think that to all intents and purposes I killed a man and yet here I lie, on this sun lounger, on this luxurious deck, with no charges hanging over me, no guilt gnawing at me, no consequences to pay. Felton, or Fenix or whatever he tried to kid himself he was called since "rising from the ashes", deserved to die. I truly believe that.

My phone rings. A familiar face flashes up on my screen.

'Hey, Allie,' says Rye on the other end.

'Hey, yourself,' I reply

'I just wanted to say happy birthday personally.'

He doesn't call me "Mum" and I don't want him to. Marla is his mum. And although Rye is his nickname, an abbreviation of his last name, Marla and Bruce honoured me enough by keeping the Christian name I gave him. They raised him well, gave him a life I could never have provided, and for that I'll always be grateful. But deeper than mother and son, there's another bond that ties Rye and I together that nobody can ever break. The truth about what happened in that graveyard, as well as the truth about what happened to Rubie and Scarlet, the Sanderson sisters, twenty-one years ago now.

I often think about them, about Rubie in particular. Rye held my hand as we sheltered in the church doorway watching paramedics wheel her towards the ambulance, still alive but unconscious. And he gripped it even tighter as Felton was zipped into a body bag. We had to give statements to the police and even through the chaos I vividly remember wondering if Rye fancied a job as a writer due to his account being such a convincing work of fiction. But he's not a writer, he has chosen to join the police, as he always wanted, via the Met's apprenticeship scheme no less. PC Ryerson. Ironic, really, but he said he wanted to be able to protect other women from men like Felton.

'I got your card last week. Thank you,' I tell him. Despite how significant last year was for both of us, I hadn't expected him to remember my birthday, what with his training and studying and adjusting to house-share life in London. But as he keeps proving, he's such a caring kid. Nothing like his father.

'You opened it early?' he asks.

'Of course. You know I don't always play by the rules.'

He laughs and I smile, still finding it extraordinary that we share the same dark sense of humour. I wouldn't have expected that when I first met him, fresh-faced and super cute in The Smugglers pub in Stonethorpe-On-Sea. He wanted to protect me even then, from Silas's raucous rant about outsiders. And how wrong old Uncle Silas was because I was always the ultimate insider.

I can sometimes still feel the heavy steel hoof cutter in my hands, the weight of it, my fingers wrapped tightly around it, not hesitating at all before swinging it against Rubie's face. She dropped to her knees, with a grunt, then fell forward against Scarlet, who tripped and face planted the ground. I moved quickly, treating her to the same punishment, making sure that both my sisters were treated equally. And then I hit them both again, blinded by rage, wanting to hurt them as much as they had hurt me, wanting to differentiate myself from them permanently.

Afterwards, I ran home. Cleaned the hoof cutter, stripped out of my blood-spattered clothes and into my pyjamas, and woke Mum up to solidify my alibi, ratting out Rubie and Scarlet for sneaking out to the party. I acted shocked and innocent when the police came knocking after their search and rescue, taking great care to hide my disappointment that both of them were still alive. I visited the hospital like a dutiful sister, only to discover that Scarlet had also been hit by a car, presumably when trying to flag down help. I'll never know if it was me or the driver that caused her brain damage.

And then, a few weeks later, as Christmas approached, my period was late. I knew I was pregnant. Felton hadn't used protection that night and all the subsequent wishing and praying and bargaining with God hadn't worked. It never had throughout my whole life, despite Mum and Uncle Silas's unwavering belief in "Him". It was the worst Christmas of my life. Even worse than the first miserable Christmas after Dad died.

My options were limited. Our household was Christian. Mum's health had deteriorated even more so she wouldn't have been able to help look after a baby even if she had wanted to. My sisters were both in hospital, not that I would ever have dreamt of depending on them for anything, least of all being doting aunties. And Silas would have built a bonfire in the back field and burned me at the stake himself.

I lived in constant fear of being found out. That plus the nausea brought on by the pregnancy made me so ill. The police had been conducting interviews with the local men, but no arrests had been made due to lack of witnesses or evidence. Journalists were still buzzing around the house and the hospital daily. Although Rubie still couldn't remember any details about the attack and Scarlet was in a coma, their conditions could have changed at any time. And either or both could have pointed the finger at me.

I had no choice but to run, and I had to go before my pregnant belly began to show. On New Year's Eve, when Uncle Silas came back to Stonethorpe for another one of his frequent visits and to take Mum to the hospital again, I packed a few things and said goodbye to the farmhouse for good. I took Mum's gold locket, some money from the secret stash under Rubie's bed, and then hitched a lift out of town. It broke my heart to leave my loving mum who had always championed me in her soft, quiet way, but who had become too unwell to control Rubie and her increasingly nasty rages. But I reasoned that having one less daughter to worry about would be better for her, and that Rubie and Scarlet needed her more than I did.

For want of anywhere better to go, I managed to get to Leeds, where I'd originally dreamed about going to university. But I experienced a very different education in the following months and years. Although my memory of that time is still sharp, the pain I felt doesn't cut as deep anymore.

'I got your gift last week too,' Rye says now. 'Signed by the author – I'm honoured. Thanks. It'll go front and centre on my bookshelf.'

'You're welcome,' I reply, touched by the pride in his voice.

Before I even finished ghostwriting the final book in the *Forgotten Fairground* series for Ralph, I began pouring all my true creativity into a new project. A tale about three sisters and the crime that tore them apart. I changed all the names, of course, twisted the truth enough to forge a work of fiction, but the heart of it remains true. The novel was published last week and it's already climbing the bestseller lists. The story that nearly destroyed me has become the story that defines me.

'Did you make that charitable donation you were considering?' Rye asks.

'I did,' I confirm. 'Not the worthiest cause but you were right – it's only fair and I do feel better for being philanthropic.'

'I told you you would.'

I smile at his cheekiness. 'How did you get so wise?'

'Marla and Bruce obviously,' he says, and I laugh. He's not

wrong though; as much as I would like to take credit for his genetics, his parents were a much better, kinder influence on him than I would have ever been. He's been making me think about a few things differently and I appreciate his alternative and thoughtful perspectives. He's got a good, logical head on his shoulders, already able to see the bigger picture.

'How's Mason?' Rye asks. 'Still treating you okay?'

'Speak of the devil,' I say as Mason appears on the deck carrying two flutes of champagne.

Mason gives me a questioning look and I mouth 'Ralph' as he hands me a glass. I don't feel bad about the lie; he doesn't know that Rye is my son yet. We've been dating since he called me last New Year's Eve with a belated Christmas present – the final piece of the puzzle. He'd found the girl who was attacked in 1998 after seeing her obituary notice online. He tracked down her husband who said she'd only ever spoken about it once. She'd bravely refused to let it define her. Her attacker? Phillip Roberts senior – her then boyfriend's father. It seems Phillip junior was cheating on Caroline with her, and his dad wanted a bit of her too. According to the husband's account, Phillip junior gaslit the poor girl into believing it was her fault. She was too ashamed to admit it, so she let the police believe it was a serial, annual crime. Obviously, it culminated in the town getting rid of the fair, which caused Phillip senior a great loss of earnings, but he got away lightly; better that than to be locked up. No wonder the Roberts were so guarded when I interviewed them. I knew there was something off about that Phillip.

When Mason told me the news, I felt strangely disappointed that Felton Clifton wasn't the guilty party of the 1998 attack. I would have bet money on it being him and I would have liked for him to be named and shamed, albeit posthumously. But he was guilty of enough. I looked him up, afterwards, under his new name. Unbelievably, he was a qualified counsellor and worked with sex offenders. And he had a wife and young daughter of his own. How fucked up is all that? I nearly choked when I saw his professional profile online, his mug shot staring back at me. The face that other rapists had looked at for guidance, the voice that other rapists had listened to for advice, as if he was even remotely worthy to counsel them. Or maybe he gave them pointers. Leopards don't change their spots, in my opinion. It still makes me sick.

'No complaints up to now,' I say in response to Rye's question about Mason, who is rapidly becoming a welcome antidote to Felton Clifton and one or two other undesirable men I was unfortunate enough to encounter in my past. 'Anyway, I'd better let you go. Keep in touch.'

'Will do,' he says. 'Bye, Allie.'

'Book sale update?' asks Mason, believing I was speaking to Ralph.

'No, he was just calling to wish me a happy birthday.'

He takes off his sunglasses. 'And is it – a happy birthday? Here with me?'

I nod and take a sip of champagne. 'I think it might just be the happiest birthday I've ever had,' I say, genuinely meaning it, even though there have also been a few men who have spoilt me rotten over the years, once I managed to navigate my way out of my vulnerable early twenties. I wasn't lying about the sugar daddies; I did what I had to do back then. I always have and I always will. I must admit that Claudia made a fuss of me too, for the one birthday of mine that we celebrated together. But this feels different. Less transactional than most of the other relationships I've had.

I idly trace the old horizontal scar tissue on my lower abdomen. Mason hasn't asked me about it yet and I'm not sure what I'll tell him when he eventually does. Maybe I'll lie but maybe I'll tell him the truth: I was so distraught at the thought of having my rapist's baby that I tried to cut myself open when I was too far gone to abort. I didn't get very far, thankfully, before my "boyfriend" at the time intervened, but the trauma caused me to give birth prematurely. Tears prick my eyes at the hideous memory of that night – the night I hit rock bottom – as well as the challenging weeks that followed. I gave birth early, too early, but Charlie was a fighter. Giving him up for adoption was both a relief and yet the most harrowing thing I have ever done. But I always kept a copy of that photo of us. It was the only time I ever held him, just before they took him away. But, unlike the saying goes: what doesn't kill you doesn't kill you. I was already stronger than I believed at the time.

I sniff and adjust my sunglasses as Mason leans down to kiss me. His lips linger on mine for a few seconds as though he knows I need comfort in this moment. Maybe he senses more than I realise, his old journalistic instincts telling him there's so much more to my story than the sketchy details I've revealed so far. Yet he never pushes, never pressures, never goes into interview mode, excavating for extra details. He's exactly what I need right now, and I can see us going the distance. He has recently accepted a new role at his old university – King's College in London – and casually suggested I move there with him, bringing Story my cat too, of course. Cutting ties with both Stonethorpe-On-Sea and Leeds feels tempting, and of course, it would mean we would both be closer to our children, perhaps become a family of sorts. Just because my original nuclear one didn't work out too well, doesn't mean a blended one won't. I'm giving it some thought. He settles on the sun lounger beside me, ready for another stunning sunset.

As the sun sinks lower, I watch the colours streak across the sky and feel a sense of peace. I no longer hear a baby crying in my dreams and no longer wake up in a cold sweat, haunted by the past or distressed by knocks on the door.

I subtly raise my glass in a private toast, smiling to myself. Scarlet still may not speak but it turns out it's me who's the silent sister. I'm the one who will never share the secret of the Sanderson attack with anyone other than my mutually silent son.

CHAPTER THIRTY-SIX

RUBIE

Rubie's head throbs. The headaches still come like clockwork, regular reminders of what happened in the graveyard a year ago. Her face and head are now scarred inside and out, and she suffers with permanent slight lag to her motor functions as a consequence, but she's alive and well, on the whole.

She presses her palms to her temples, cradling her head in her hands, feeling the slight indent on the right side of her skull. Dot has informed her it's barely noticeable but that's because Rubie still wears her hair over that side of her face. It's shorter now though – a sleek shoulder-length bob influenced by a model from an old *Just Seventeen* magazine, which Rubie happened upon after finally hunting out Scarlet's other diaries. It seems her sister enjoyed scrapbooking too, especially crudely defacing images of Rubie. She wouldn't have been surprised to have found a voodoo doll of herself too. But anyway, she was happy about the hair inspiration because the bob makes her feel sexy and sophisticated.

Rubie reaches for the box of tablets and the glass of water on her bedside table. The strong medication helps to dull the sharpness of the pain, but they often leave her a bit groggy. Still, needs must. She swallows one, sets the glass back down and leans against her headboard, thinking about the day ahead. It's her birthday. Thirty-eight years old. She made it.

She closes her eyes, her thoughts drifting back to last year. Rosalie's venomous voice, the cold concrete of her mother's headstone, falling into a deep, black, unconscious hole. She was surprised to wake up again, to find herself in hospital. For a split-second she thought it was still 1997. It took weeks for her to reorient herself, to make sense of the fragments she remembered. She's still not sure she has recalled it all as it really was; the doctors told her that her headaches would cause "glitches" in her memory. Her new therapist, however, has described it as "trauma-blocking" – her brain protecting itself. She has a sense that a younger man was there that day but for the life of her she still doesn't know who he was. Maybe just someone visiting a grave who got caught up in all the drama.

But she does know now that Felton died that day. She seems to think she had a question to ask him, but it escapes her now. It can't have been that important.

The house is unusually quiet. Scarlet must still be asleep. Their relationship has changed significantly since Rubie found her first diary last year, the day that their bond initially broke. Since finding her other diaries, that bond is now irreparable. She no longer trusts Scarlet, no longer believes that her sister was, or is, her best friend. And if Scarlet is still mentally sixteen years old, then she must still hate Rubie as much as she did then. Well, the feeling is mutual.

Scarlet's betrayal still stings so badly that they now have separate bedrooms – Rubie has moved into Rosalie's old room – and lead separate lives within the farmhouse. Silas still presides over them, but not as menacingly or aggressively as before, thankfully. Mandated AA meetings and his renewed commitment to religion, both courtesy of the vicar's welcome intervention last year, have helped reduce his violent outbursts but he's still gruff and difficult at times. It's an improvement though, and Rubie's grateful for small mercies.

She swings her legs out of bed and plants her feet on the floor. Now that the tablet is starting to kick in, she takes her phone out of her bedside drawer. Sometimes she struggles to focus on the small screen due to intermittent vision issues but today it's manageable. She sees that she has a couple of new orders on her pet supplies website, which cheers her immensely. Her hard work over the past few months in building the business online has been paying off and she's now earning a few hundred pounds a month. A third notification catches her eye and Rubie gasps. It's a direct donation of £5,000. She checks the sender's name: *A. Sawyer*. Rubie knits her brows together, knowing there's something familiar about it. Ah yes, it's her recurring weekly customer who places the same £50 order every week. They've been her saving grace and now this. She clicks on the notification and navigates to the donation page. There's a message attached:

Happy birthday. Allie x

Rubie's jaw drops. A. Sawyer is Allie – Rosalie. She's the one behind all the orders. Why? Some sort of blood money or a compensation of sorts for what she did last year – speaking to Rubie so cruelly? She can certainly remember them physically fighting but the exact reason why is still hazy. Their usual deep-seated sister grievances, no doubt. A spark of anger ignites within Rubie, but it soon snuffs itself out. She can't deny the impact her sister's most recent actions have had on her life. Without that confrontation and her injury in the graveyard, the vicar wouldn't have helped her speak to social services, and without that, they would never have been assigned a carer, and without that, Rubie wouldn't have been able to begin online counselling. She might never have found Dr Richards.

Her cheeks flush as she thinks of him. Her therapist. Her saviour. Their weekly online sessions have become the highlight of her life. His velvet voice is like a soothing balm for her soul. His handsome face is now more dear to her than the boy band posters still Blu-Tacked to the wall in the bedroom she and Scarlet used to share. She fantasises about him often, about meeting him in person one day. In her daydreams he's her perfect man: kind, understanding, blind to her scars, and deeply in love with her. Everything she once hoped Felton Clifton would be.

Scarlet doesn't know about Dr Richards and Rubie intends to keep it that way. Dot and the carer Corinne always make sure she has absolute privacy for their sessions, keeping Scarlet entertained elsewhere in the house. Occasionally Rubie can hear banging or things breaking and knows that Scarlet is acting out again, hating the fact that she's no longer her sister's focus, but she's learnt to simply ignore her now.

No, Dr Richards is a secret she guards fiercely, making sure that Scarlet doesn't see the effort she goes to for their video calls either. It's been fun for Rubie, blow-drying her new bob, wearing a bit of make-up again, wearing pretty clothes, enjoying his appreciative smile when she pops onto the screen. She's sure she's not imagining their deep connection and feels certain that it's only a matter of time before he admits his true feelings and they progress from doctor and patient to boyfriend and girlfriend. He understands her like nobody ever has and given her hope for a happy future again. *Mrs Rubie Richards definitely has a nice ring to it*, she thinks.

Rubie ventures downstairs to the kitchen where the table is set for breakfast for one. A red envelope with her name on it lays on her placemat. She picks it up, knowing instantly who it's from. Inside she finds a card emblazoned with the message *Happy Birthday to a Special Sister*. Below the swirly, saccharine verse Scarlet has written one word: *Sorry*. Dot or Corinne must have got it from the post office for her. Rubie scowls. Too little, too late. She rips up the card and throws it in the bin, envelope and all. Sometimes she wishes she had been the one to bash Scarlet's head in as they crossed the field that night. If she'd have known back then how much her supposed beloved sister despised her, she might well have done.

'You're up,' states Dot as she bustles in from outside. Oak and Elm are hot on her heels following their usual morning jaunt out in the back field. Rubie loves that they're all in a routine now, the household working like a fine-tuned engine, the pressure finally off her.

'Happy birthday,' says the older woman, as brisk as ever, while she sets about hanging up her jacket then breaking eggs in a bowl.

'Thanks,' says Rubie.

Dot glances at her as she whisks. 'Get your card?'

Rubie nods but offers no explanation as to why Scarlet's card isn't now displayed on top of the table. It's none of Dot's business as Rubie told her in no uncertain terms a while back. It felt good to be assertive and Dot hasn't directly alluded to the sisters' estrangement ever since, although she must wonder what went wrong between them, considering they were practically conjoined. Or maybe she doesn't wonder, doesn't give it a second thought. Either way, Rubie doesn't care. She takes great pleasure in being utterly selfish these days.

While Dot cooks her breakfast, Rubie fusses the dogs, her mind returning to Allie and her £5,000 donation. It's a sizeable sum. Perhaps enough for cosmetic surgery to tidy up her scar. It might even be enough for driving lessons and a little car so she can finally meet Dr Richards for face-to-face sessions, although she'd have to get her headaches under control first. But it's certainly enough for a bus or train ticket to Leeds to surprise Dr Richards in person. And funnily enough, maybe she'll be able to engineer a little catch-up with Allie too. Her P.O. Box is a Leeds address so there's a good chance that's where she now lives. Rubie would love to thank her for her generosity, for supporting her business, and suggest that more of that would ensure she stays silent about what happened in the graveyard last year. Not that Rubie can remember all of it – yet – but the very fact that Allie has chosen to send this donation implies she's paying Rubie for something. Rubie may be slightly slower than she was in some respects, but she isn't stupid.

She smiles widely as Dot serves up scrambled eggs, fresh from the silkies outside.

'Thank you,' she says, meaning it, because she is thankful. Thankful for all she's set to gain after everything she's lost. It's about time.

THE END

ALSO BY C.L. JENNISON

The Desperate Wife

What's Mine is Yours

Sunday's Child

More Fool Me

ACKNOWLEDGEMENTS

Thank you, as always, to the fantastic team at Bloodhound Books, especially Tara and Ian. I feel so lucky to have found a home in the Bloodhound kennel.

Special thanks go to my husband Richard, not just for being my staunchest supporter, but also for suggesting that I start setting my novels somewhere a bit more exotic than Yorkshire (or a fictional town within it), so that we could maybe enjoy a few 'research' trips. Your wish is my command: anything for the good of the books!

Thank you to the wider Jennison family too, who always take such an interest in my stories. With permission, I named two of the characters in this book Caroline and Phillip, after my in-laws. But let me be clear: that's where the similarities end!

The erstwhile fair featured in *The Silent Sister* is an amalgamation of two places very close to my heart: Pleasure Island near my home town of Grimsby, which I frequented during my teenage summers in the 90s, and Hull Fair, which I've visited many times since moving to Hull permanently about fifteen years ago. Thankfully, my fond memories of both are far more pleasant than what unfolds in the book...

And finally, thank you to you for picking up and reading this story. I hope *The Silent Sister* kept you guessing and gave you a few delicious thrills along the way.

A NOTE FROM THE PUBLISHER

Thank you for reading this book. If you enjoyed it please do consider leaving a review on Amazon to help others find it too.

We hate typos. All of our books have been rigorously edited and proofread, but sometimes mistakes do slip through. If you have spotted a typo, please do let us know and we can get it amended within hours.

info@bloodhoundbooks.com